Blood and Milk

Blood and Milk

STORIES

Sharon Solwitz

Sarabande Books
LOUISVILLE, KENTUCKY

Copyright © 1997 by Sharon Solwitz

Managing Editor
Sarabande Books, Inc.
2234 Dundee Road, Suite 200
Louisville, KY 40205

LIBRARY OF CONGRESS CATALOGING-IN-PUBLICATION DATA

Solwitz, Sharon, 1945–
    Blood and milk : stories / by Sharon Solwitz. – 1st ed.
        p. cm.
    Contents: Blood – The country of herself – Obst vw – Small talk
– Editing – The hand is not ironic – Fossilized – Mercy – If you
step on a crack – Milk – Polio.
    ISBN 1-889330-01-9 (cloth : alk. paper). – ISBN 1-889330-02-7
(pbk. : alk. paper).
    I. Title.
PS3569.06514B57 1997
813' .54–dc20
                                     96-44142 CIP

Cover painting: *Wally in Red Blouse with Raised Knees,* 1913, by Egon Schiele.
Gouache, watercolor and pencil, 12 ½" x 18 ⅞". Reproduced with
the kind permission of Serge Sabarsky, Inc., New York, New York.

Cover and interior design by Charles Casey Martin.

Manufactured in the United States of America.
This book is printed on acid-free paper.

Sarabande Books is a nonprofit literary organization.

for Barry,
with love

Acknowledgments

American Short Fiction, "The Hand Is Not Ironic."

The Chicago Tribune, "Polio"; "The Country of Herself"; the latter reprinted in *The Country of Herself*, Third Side Press.

The Chicago Tribune Magazine, "Blood."

Manoa, "Fossilized."

Other Voices, "Editing."

Playgirl, "Milk."

Ploughshares, "OBST VW"; reprinted in Stephen Minot's *Three Genres*, 5th ed., Prentice Hall.

Tikkun, "If You Step on a Crack."

"Small Talk" originally appeared in *Stand*, 1991.

"Mercy" originally appeared in *TriQuarterly*, a publication of Northwestern University Press; reprinted in *Pushcart Prize: Best of the Small Presses*, 1996.

I would like to thank the following organizations for their encouragement, financial and spiritual: the Heekin Foundation, the Illinois Arts Council, and the Ragdale Foundation.

Thanks also to my friends and teachers for their help and encouragement: Rosellen Brown, Tsivia Cohen, Garry Cooper, Pamela Erbe, Alan Friedman, Robin Hemley, Lore Segal, Sarah Skolnik, James Park Sloan, Gene Wildman, Joyce Winer, and Sandi Wisenberg.

Contents

❦ Blood ❦

I'm thirty-five, reasonably attractive, and bright enough not to believe in the existence of a perfect anything, but I can't stop thinking about this donor. The guy had lovely veins that swelled at the first twist of the tourniquet. He didn't wince at the prick, in fact complimented my gentle hands. I loved his left hand, awkward, careful rolling up his sleeve, and the way his arm swelled into his sleeve, and his smell of tea and salt, and the Boston way he flattened out his final *r*'s. Stretched out on the table with his blood streaming up into one of our pint jars he fainted, passed out (it happens sometimes), and when he woke up he gave me a look so straight my eyes melted, I couldn't look back. But I didn't ask his name, all I know about him is he's kicking around an empty house (that's how he said it) and that he wants his blood to go to leukemia children.

In fantasy A, he's new in Chicago, divorced perhaps as a result of losing his kid to that awful disease. Counseled, they wept together but couldn't get over it, and the compassion he learned as a result of his loss has rendered him, if not perfect for me, at least the best fit after ten years of trying for a fit. And he's gone into the wilderness along with all the men I should have turned down in high school and college and beyond.

For the rest of the day I'm sloppy, numb to the angle of vein, the thickness of skin and vascular wall. People flinch, glare at me. A pale, thin, blond young woman asks, "How long have you been doing this?" Larry, a fellow technician with whom I've been nurturing a bloodless friendship, looks at me as if he's worried about me, but I'm too upset to feel further upset. That I registered our commonality and let him go: It's more proof of my curse, to be forever alone–I've thought a lot about this here at the blood bank. There are very few men I can fruitfully mate with. It's a genetic trait like red hair, trouble with math; like your blood type. Some people are O, universal donors, everybody loves them. Some people are AB, universal receivers, they can love just about anybody. But I require a mix of strength and delicacy so polar they do not coexist in the human psyche, and the reviews are mixed as to what I offer in return. I'm transfused Rh negative, my antibodies have antibodies. I'm some rare type that only gets called for once in a blue moon, and then of course it's been used up on someone who died and there's nothing in stock.

I IMAGINE I'LL STOP THINKING about him when I get home. I'll take a bubble bath. Wheel the set over to the bathroom so I can watch the news under a blanket of bubbles, then get in bed with *How to Score High on the GRE's* and do analogies till my eyes fall shut. Archipelago is to island as 1) club : member; 2) country : state; 3) family : individual. I darken number 3, without reading

[4]

the rest, try to envision my satisfying future life as a biologist or professor of biology. But a wave of Boston assails me, not his face, which has faded into the blur of all handsome faces, but the feel of his hand on my arm as I helped him sit up, the way I imagine his hand on my arm. And from upstairs I hear: Jean-Paul and Simone are at it again.

I call them Jean-Paul and Simone, though I mean of course the ordinary people in the apartment above me. I've seen them only a handful of times, talked to him once, her, never, but I know his real name from the mailbox (A. Morandi), I know their cars, I know when they're home, and I know from the precise aural quality of their lovemaking how well they're getting along from day to day.

Sometimes they do it on the couch. Then I get a few muffled moans, maybe a soft thump as they fall conjoined (I imagine) to the floor—their living room is carpeted. But their bedroom is not. The worst is when she comes in late at night. He keeps normal hours, he runs a store—office supplies, I think, from the boxes on his back seat—but she's a flight attendant, and some nights, at three or four in the morning, here she comes in her high heels down their hard-wood hallway right over my hallway—spick spick spick—then off with the shoes—thuck thuck—and then it's bedspring city. He pants, she squeals—my God, they haven't seen each other for forty-eight hours! Forty-eight hours without body touch, skin on skin! Though to tell you the truth I'm not sure how fully she enjoys it. Those yowls seem a little canned; too even, if you know what I mean, the same pitch and frequency night after night. In the serving profes-sions it's hard to let go, I guess, wheeling the beverage cart, lying in bed ever ready for the call, *Miss?*

He does his best for her, though, in my informed opinion—thirty to thirty-five minutes minimum. I shouldn't have timed it but sometimes you're your own worst enemy, and anyway what else to do at four of a winter morning when it's too cold to get out of bed but stare at the red glowing transformations of your digital clock?

In bed now I turn my electric blanket on, though I've heard the current impairs your immune system, and imagine myself like her, warm under his weight. In her place, I imagine, I would burst open, unfurl into a bouquet of velvet flowers. And I remember what my friend Moira said after she quit waitressing and got all at once that great job with a company car and a company lover to boot (albeit married)—that the trick is admitting to yourself you *want* something. For women, says Moira, this is especially hard. For women, simple wanting is troublesome, since, despite lib et al., all we really feel comfortable about having is what fate or some authority figure casts our way. So I lie in bed saying to myself, I want you, Jean-Paul. I want you, my man with the Boston accent, the beautiful strong hands; the hands of a carpenter, I imagine. He does elegant work, I imagine. Originally a lawyer, he had never liked it, the low hum of corruption, so that when his younger brother died after years of pain and chemotherapy, he said, No more. Life is short! "Life is short!" I murmur, a mental cry of desire that will tap his shoulder, take his hand, and draw him to me.

I'm awakened first by my father on the phone, his voice taut with enthusiasm for my plans for graduate school as if I'll change my mind if he lets up.

I'm awakened later by a scream that I think is mine until my dream collapses. Upstairs, Jean-Paul is shouting at Simone. There are scraping sounds, as if furniture is being moved, then a thud too soft for furniture. Visible against the window, my hanging plant sways slightly. Some words come through, hers, not his: "Just cut that out!" "If you come near me—!" Her voice is shrill, trembly, fluttering like flaps of broken balloon at each blast from Jean-Paul, who has been reduced to simple noise, he has lost his human component, and I turn on the light, reach for my study guide. Archipelago is to island as 4) sentence : word.

I had a boyfriend who slapped me once, grabbed my hair and slapped my face.

My stomach hurts as her heels spick spick down the hall and the door whoomfs shut behind her.

AT WORK I'M LANGUID with too little sleep, sliding needle into vein as slowly and tenderly as a lover. Donors gaze at me with the too-open eyes of virgins winningly caressed in private places. "You're good at this," says a curly-haired, soft-voiced perhaps violin student, who tells me he's selling his blood to pay for his date tonight. Like a geisha I lower my eyes over the alcohol swab as I withdraw the prick.

But today I cannot bear men. My buddy Larry asks me to lunch, and I tell him no. Larry is ten years younger than I and he drives me home if there's nothing better in town for either of us to do and once he played me a recording of "Bolero" into which he'd spliced a woman's augmenting sighs—did he think it would turn me on? "Got to work," I say, tapping my study guide.

"I'll buy," says Larry, peering over my shoulder at the page I'm working on. "I speak your language," he says. "Male is to female as 1) passion is to resistance; 2) love is to fear—"

"Dumb is to dumber," I say to the numbers on the page. Thinking of my frail-boned Simone, wobbly on her high heels. Of Jean-Paul, not Jean-Paul anymore, just A. Morandi, a dull-witted blaster, a simple, ordinary man who permits himself the luxury of losing control of himself.

"You know your problem?" says Moira over the phone. "You don't want anyone real. You want a phantom man."

"I don't want any men," I say. "I want you."

"You should go out with Larry," she says firmly. Since therapy she has become certain of many things. "For practice. He really likes you."

"Practice makes perfect," I say.

"Rennie, you are so *hostile!*"

"A barbed wire fence," I reply. "A stone wall."

In the pause I can hear the hum of Moira's perfectly oiled psyche, in which there is no disjunction between thought and action. "My therapist says," she says in her too loud voice, "if you haven't been disappointed at least three times a day you haven't been trying!"

"Fire him, Moira. Save yourself."

Still her advice stays around, sits on the table in front of me, sure of itself as winter boots. Or maybe I'm just empowered by my own smartassery: I call up the computer file of yesterday's donors. There are sixty-seven entries, mostly male, none of whom practice behavior associated with the AIDS virus.

I'm ripping off the sheet of continuous-feed paper when Larry returns from lunch, sweet and rodent-like. He leans over my desk, accepts my apology. Is somehow stimulated by my apology to ask me to dinner tonight.

Oh, Larry, save yourself. Oh, Larry, I would chew you at dinner into little rodent pieces. "I'm sorry," I say. Turning away to the printout as if the man exists somehow in the letters of his name: Jeffrey K. Allen. Andrew Blaha. Michael Howard Brustein. He's a psychiatrist, perhaps. Not one of those troubled souls who went into it to figure himself out, but a shrink with a calling, a sort of atheist rabbi, who would have gone to rabbinical school if he could have worshiped a god nasty enough to create diseases like childhood leukemia.

HOME EARLY, I sink onto my couch with my study guide open across my waist like an apron. The phone rings, and I follow each arc of sound, rising, falling. Happy am I without the footfalls of A. Morandi and his flight attendant. Happy am I pressing into the crack of my couch. Outside, the snow is falling white and soft, blurring and hushing the city street. Inside is the hum of the fridge, the serene knocking of the radiator deciding whether or not to dispense heat, a faint skittering in the wall that might be a mouse, a roach. Archipelago is to island as family of roaches is to an individual roach.

At five-thirty as usual my neighbor's car squeals to a stop against the curb (it needs a brake job). It's as if I can see him through the walls, A. Morandi, burly-armed from lifting those boxes, heavy-footed. I pull an afghan down from the back of the couch as he thumps up the linoleum stairs, thwooshes open his door.

I'm shivering; can't stop. My boyfriend, a proud and sensitive young man, would hit me for acts that knicked his sensitive pride. He used a belt once, I remember, and the buckle knicked me, and there was blood on the back of my skirt, blood down the back of my leg, I remember, or do I? I hear him distinctly in my mind saying he didn't mean it. He or someone whispers, kneels, kisses the back of my knee, and the whispery voice has his inflections, and I feel his day's beard on the skin of the back of my leg. And I'm assailed by wisps of images of pain and pleasure mixed up together, myself wrapped in something too wispy vague for a name though it has something in common with terror—archipelago is to island as history is to event, as memory is to wisp of fading image—and I lie stiff as a victim waiting for A. Morandi's steps across the kitchen tile, the slight bang as he opens his refrigerator door too hard and it hits the wall.

But the footsteps of A. Morandi are soft on his living room rug. He turns on the answering machine, and I hear distinctly—shrill, bright, apologetic, "Hi, it's me in Pittsburgh! We're stuck, nothing is leaving here, what a job! Oh, Angelo, we need to talk. Ange, you were right. But you were wrong. Well. This is stupid. Ange, I love you. I'll call you later. Or call me, but don't scream, okay?"

She leaves her Marriott number. Her voice sounds awkward to me, unlovely, but he plays it over and over. Ange, I love you. He puts his hand to his mouth. Wraps his arms around himself. His burly arms around his tender self.

I call Larry, describe my Boston man in terms of height, build, eye color, how he walked, how he carried his fine head on his neck, his unthinkable mix of violence and kindness, violence transmuted by kindness into something impossibly fine and strong, but Larry, who could place every woman under the age of fifty as late as seventy-two hours after she walked out of the clinic, has no recollection. "That's all right," I say. "That's fine. You're sweet, Larry, you know that?"

It is all right. I retrieve the computer paper from my purse, dial the first number, Jeffrey Allen's. Oh, love, I will say. I took your blood but you got some of mine too. Who are you?

❦ The Country of Herself ❦

The sidewalk is wide enough for four to walk abreast but the man passes so close his arm brushes her arm. Too light for a jostle, too quick for sleaze, but she feels stung. It has happened to her before, this piece of foreign rudeness, in this same dress so long and loose it's almost a chador, but not with baby Ike in his pack around her neck. She lifts the front pack and airs her chest, then kisses the brim of his little blue hat. Perhaps it has to do with what she read in the paper this morning, Israel's capture of an important Muslim cleric. Or her red hair flaming out from all these covered heads. Her arms in her short sleeves? The sensation lingers on the back of her arm like a bug bite. She says to her husband, "Win, I am hating this place."

"What place do you like?"

"Oh stop."

The man's *khafiyeh,* loose white shirt, and incongruous European-style vest blur into a group of similar outfits. The air over the street is hot and damp, too thick to breathe let alone talk through. She argues inside herself. Jerusalem she loved for the smell of the stone, and London for the constant motion of the streets, and Madison, Wisconsin, where she met Win and married him, for the light wind that made her skin hum with the pleasure of feeling. In Baghdad the wind blows a gray-yellow dust tinting the windows and sidewalks and the men's white pajama suits and even the skin of her arms. In Baghdad your skin isn't yours, she feels, but the property of the insects and men about town who desire it. Wear long sleeves. Do not scratch no matter how bad the itch. Breathe lightly.

THAT'S HOW SHE TALKS, simple words, hardly any accent. But he has to think about what she says and even then he isn't sure he has it figured out. She walks a half-step ahead of him, always faster than he walks: Dvora Wallace née Blank. Fill in the Blank, he sometimes says to her, a joke. In pain there's an element of Blank, she once said. From Emily Dickinson. A little grim, but her style, *her* joke, he thinks. Baghdad is no worse, ladies and gentlemen of the jury, than some of the other places they've lived. Despair is her dramatic art, statements like all she wants of a place is the right to go crazy without anyone staring. Not that it's exactly easy here for her, being Israeli, but they aren't planning to spend their lives, probably not more than another year. She simply likes to startle. It gives her power at dinner parties, though it bothers some people, himself included. "Why do you talk like that?" he said to her once, explaining that it came across to him and many people as intentionally cryptic. And she said with anger at the bottom of her voice that she didn't know "many people" and it was not at all "cryptic" (sneering at his word) for people whose minds weren't spoiled by all day sucking up to assholes. Not fair, he still thinks. Or at least there are kinder ways to put it. He knows how to use warmth and persistence and the velvety edge of power dealing with folks not born to Western ways of business—getting utilities hooked up, for example, by native service people for whom contracts are as binding as New Year's resolutions, and at the end they still like him, the company heads and the native contractors; nothing to be ashamed of. He's happy till he has a good reason not to be and he doesn't mess with other people's good moods. "I try to be tactful," he said to Dvora. To which she replied, "Your mind is spoiled by tact." Now what was that supposed to mean?

THE ITCH IS UNDER THE PACK, between her breasts, where she cannot scratch. She wonders whether it's an old itch or a new one in the making. Either way there's nothing she can do. Baby Ike wakes up and starts to cry.

"He's hungry," Win says.

"He cannot be hungry," she says. She'd nursed him in the apartment half an hour ago. She puts his pacifier back in his mouth.

"He's so white," Win says. "Do you think he's sick?"

"He is not sick." She lifts the brim of his baby hat. On his temple, showing pale blue through the skim milk-colored skin is a pattern of veins radiating out from a circle like a child's drawing of the sun. "It's your shadow," she says. "His skin looks blue in your shadow over him."

Win bends down and kisses Ike's cheek with so much force the baby squawks. She inserts the pacifier a second time. "Your kiss is a punch sometimes," she says. "A left to the jaw!" She pats Win's cheek, demonstrating how to touch softly, although as far as she knows, he doesn't feel light touches. To arouse him she must do to him what would cause her pain. Sometimes she thinks he has no nerve endings in his skin. "I will dye my hair brown," she says.

"Please don't."

"I want something to eat," she says.

"It's Ramadan, there's no place open."

"Even when it is not Ramadan."

One of the things she hates about Baghdad is the near total absence of restaurants. Although she isn't really hungry. She just wants something like padding over her nerve endings, which feel too exposed. Alongside this main street and affixed to many of the buildings are larger-than-life paintings of a mustached man in various costumes, the country's president, staring at her. The street is crowded with men who stare at her, and though they do not speak or gesture she feels their feeling for her, their what-would-be loathing if she were significant enough to loathe. If she weren't an infidel and a woman. A Jewish woman in a country where Jews (the 300 remaining) aren't allowed to own their homes. A Jewish woman from a country that, unprovoked, bombed a nuclear plant in this country, reported to be making bombs and not electricity, and although she wasn't convinced—had in fact written a letter deploring the attack, which the *Post* had printed—it wouldn't have helped her get a visa. Jewish tourists can't get visas here—Jews and people with AIDS, she has discovered; five days after they arrived they'd had to take an AIDS test, which did not, thank God, expose her nationality. On her application she'd lied about her nationality, also her religion, her father's name, her grandfather's name; carrying her visa now she sometimes wonders who she is. No one knows she's Jewish-Israeli, but it's hard enough being a Western woman, perhaps significant enough or something enough to be taken hostage and traded for the newly captured Muslim cleric. "I need a chador," she says.

"You'd look silly in a chador."

Actually, she doesn't want a chador, which stands for a good part of what appalls her. Actually, she wants to tear off her clothes and scratch where she isn't allowed to scratch, her crotch, and under her milk-heavy breasts. "A chador would hide my hair," she says.

"Let's go back to the apartment."

"The apartment is death."

"Do you want me to carry the baby? I'll be glad to."

"He's fine where he is."

"You have great hair," he says. "It would be a sin to hide your hair."

He works to humor her, but out of selfishness, she thinks, to protect his own good mood. She holds his arm even though she's angry with him. She is so often angry with him she can't afford to act on it anymore. So she holds him fiercely. Calls him sweet names. Feels her anger in her eyes, making ugly things uglier, the greasy dust on the bolts of fabric in the store window she is passing. And maybe also, her anger, on her wrists and ankles that itch so intensely now it feels like burning. The sun eats through the opaque white sky, burning her arms, her head through her hair, the tops of her feet around the leather thongs of her sandals. Clumsy around the front pack, she's rummaging through her bag for her sunblock when a man pushes by on the storefront side of the walk, his sleeve glancing across her arm. "Shit, Win! They are doing it on purpose!"

"Let's go over to the Sheraton," Win says. "We can sit in the coffee shop."

"I want to go back to America. Why cannot they send you where is respect for women?" She mocks her own fluency. Two men walking in front of them stop, turn. "Mind your fucking business!" she says.

"It's a good thing they don't speak English," Win says.

"Why do you not talk to them? Apologize to them for my hot head?"

The men continue to stare at her, stock still on the sidewalk, holding onto each other's hands, with an impassivity that transcends, or so it seems, the language barrier. She makes a face at them. They do not respond.

"I think they are autistic," she says loudly.

Win pulls her away from them, whispering, "Do you want to start a fight?"

"I want *you* to start a fight, Mister America."

He squeezes her hand. "Try and calm down, Dvora. Let's go back to the apartment and play gin rummy."

She looks him dead in the eye. "My skin itches. Do you understand? I want to take it off and throw it in the fire and burn it."

He says something she doesn't hear. The dusty wind is blowing, the *shamal,* the dry northwest wind that never stops. She runs back to the store with the bolts of cloth in the window and buys enough for a chador.

HE WAITS IN THE SUN patiently like an ox. He thinks of himself as an ox; he can take physical pain, extremes of hot and cold. Once he'd wanted to be an astronaut. But Dvora weighs on him. He feels her unhappiness as strain in one of his shoulders.

Not that he blames her. The people on the street act like assholes at times. But she struts her unhappiness so that it spills over onto him, not to mention the people who have invited them into their homes: good people, at worst a little close-mouthed, who've gone out of their way to make him and Dvora feel comfortable. His only problem with them is that they don't appreciate his style of joke. Once he made a kidding remark about their street art, all those faces of Big Brother Hussein (counting, one afternoon, he'd reached 250, honest to God) making it hard for him to run a stoplight. Not ha-ha-funny maybe, but no one had even smiled.

He takes off his sport coat, shakes off the dust, then puts it back on, a little annoyed with Dvora now. He didn't force her to come here. They could have gone to Lahore or Copenhagen; Baghdad was her choice despite the official anti-Semitism. She called it "the land of my fathers." She wanted to find the Iraq beneath Iraq, the Iraq of the Bible, where Abraham was born, married, heard the word of the Jewish God and demolished the idols. There was something for her to discover here. She had said that fiercely, forehead shining. He'd imagined that if he touched her at that moment her skin would burn him.

. . .

SHE STANDS IN THE DOORWAY of the fabric shop while Win helps her drape the black swatch over her head and shoulders. The shape is wrong, she thinks—too rectangular. And it needs a hem. And she has to hold the sides together and out from below her chin so Ike can breathe. But despite the heat and the baby's weight on her neck, in the shelter of the makeshift chador she seems to float along the street, as if whatever happens from now on is happening to someone not her. *"Bella, bella,"* Win says. *"Azeh yofee!"*

She takes one edge of the fabric between her teeth like the veiled women in Damascus—a frame for their dark eyes, long straight noses, thin upper lips.

"I must have you," Win whispers.

She laughs. The fabric slips from her mouth and falls to the ground behind her. Win restores it.

"Let's go back to the apartment," he says.

"In a little," she says. "I need the exercise."

"I'll give you some exercise."

Part of her wants to comply, to feed this small burst of his feeling for her. But she likes her own feeling of being in costume, even in the narrowing streets, the thickening crowds of the old covered market they are nearing. "Ike is enjoying our walk," she says.

"Ike is sleeping," Win says.

"He will wake up when we remove him from the pack."

She kisses Win's neck as a small apology, then puts her lips to the configuration of veins on Ike's temple, so delicate that sometimes even lips seem too forceful, and only when she looks up does she notice the crowd that has gathered around them. It's made up entirely of men, and perhaps five deep already, clotting into a circle.

"Keep moving," Win says. "Toward the apartment."

He puts his arm around her shoulders, John Wayne Wallace; she can tell he's scared. She is not scared; she's looking for the words to shoo these people away. The words refuse to assemble, though; maybe she is nervous, a little. There isn't much room in the eye of their personal hurricane, eight or ten feet, the radius of the circle free of mustached men in *khafiyehs* and loose white pants, in vests scavenged, maybe, from the business suits of Western hostages. The scavengers don't speak, not even to murmur to each other. They simply move along as *they* move along, staring, not at Win but at her—hair, face, bare arms—worse than disapprovingly, the way a child stares at a cripple or a dwarf. She feels a pulse of almost-fear but doesn't try to cast it off—it seems to relieve her skin's itching, her rage at these men, who will stone a woman to death for adultery, guiltlessly, self-righteously, enacting the will of a God who guiltlessly, self-righteously ordains the woman's death for that crime but not the man's. She stares back brazenly now—she is not a Muslim woman—and slips out from under Win's arm. And as she removes herself, as she takes a step unattached, with her infant son but free of her husband, a man in white, who looks like all the other men in white, breaks the circle and pulls off her chador.

She screams. Baby Ike starts crying. She screams in Hebrew, her first language, "Give me it, you fucking fruit-bastard!" yelling as she shoves him from behind. It's a controlled shove, not enough to make him fall, just enough to register her anger, but his body, soft, falls back with surprising ease into the crowd. She watches, amazed for a moment at the power of her hands. She wants to see his face. She wants to see what she has made him feel. What of her has registered on him. Embarrassment, perhaps? Humiliation? No emotion that she can fathom. With a blank face, hardly looking at her, he takes a step toward her and spits. At her. On her. On the pleated front of this white linen dress she will never wear again. She's screaming words she has never used, Arab curses she always knew but would have been punished for using at home.

"Dvora, stop!" Win cries.

She pauses a second, waiting for him to do something–she isn't sure what–one of the violent things he must have learned from American television. But his face looks wounded and spit-at as she is sure hers is not. She picks up the chador and cleans her dress with it like a rag; then casting it away, she pushes through the crowd, which closes behind her like the door of a house she has left forever. She's not scared at all running with Ike against her chest, running fast, zigzagging down alleys like an Arab boy who has thrown stones, although she was the one stoned, no?, and running for her life with Ike thumping in his front pack, till the streets widen and empty and she has him alone.

BUT DVORA LIKED TO RUN OFF. From movies, the houses of friends, from fancy restaurants. It was not unusual. If he said something wrong, that didn't come up to the intensity of her own feeling, she'd get up from the table and leave him alone with his food. The first time he didn't even pay the check; he jumped up and ran after her. The second time he put a bill on the table, catching up to her near their apartment in Madison; it took a while to calm her down. The third time he finished his dinner, coming home to find her so enraged she threw a shoe at him and drove off in their car. He would have called the police if he hadn't known she wanted him to call the police, had choreographed that dance in order to make him.

Later, weeping, she described to him how she'd driven round and round and round the block. But, ladies and gentlemen of the jury, he says, is he responsible for that? There was something awry in the way she processed information. According to a theory he heard, the presence of the enemy—all those Arabs pressing in on that long hallway of a country—was supposed to diminish the personal ego, unite citizens in service of a common cause. But Dvora was as self-absorbed as any American he knew. Clearly she was spoiled; her family extra-privileged, dad official consul to the American Midwest—doors open for her; mucho cultural glitz. And then her personal early glory—an IQ called off the charts, with subsequent inordinate respect from adults. But every year or two her mother would go "vague" (Dvora's word) and vanish for a while to some fancy sanitarium—maybe she didn't get enough love, or enough of the right kind of love?

He walks away from the window, the dusty gray-green of the trees in the little park across the street, hearing Dvora's response. "Amateur psychology." She threw that at him once. "Puerile analysis." Probably it is. It doesn't make him any happier with his wife, who, for whatever reason, seems to perceive her half of anything as the smaller portion. Dvora, the Israeli, from the place God picked out for the people He picked out of all the peoples of the earth. How was an ordinary gentile supposed to respond to that? What about his feelings, his stomach in knots at restaurants and movies, since a chance remark, what failure on his part to laugh or cry at the right time would bring on the big guns? He feels bad for not having managed to find her on the streets of Baghdad, worse than bad, but she's a grown woman with a will and a temper that can lay him flat—he shouldn't have to take all the blame.

SHE IS ALMOST EUPHORIC on the anonymous street, a feeling she hasn't had in so long it makes her throat tight. Directly across from her and behind a little stone bench is a portrait of the Iraqi president with a smile on his face, kissing the hand of someone's baby. Seated on the bench two head-scarfed young men with hard, handsome jaws vie for the honor of directing her to the train station, their Arabic as clear and pure as Hebrew to her ears.

Her elation continues on the train, although there are no empty seats, and the windows are so grimy she can barely see out. Ike, asleep around her neck, seems to weigh nothing at all. There are women on the train—perhaps a third of the passengers, and the first she has seen with animated faces. Within the shelter of their chadors they are talking to each other, unlike the women who hurry along the city streets looking straight out in front of them like horses. These women might answer her if she asked them a question. They might forgive her bare arms and tell her the address of a good jewelry shop, the name of a responsible person to help with the baby. That they don't look at her now doesn't feel hostile for some reason; she is an outsider here but not an enemy. None of the

men offer her their seat but that doesn't seem hostile either, not
even rude, simply innocent. Their innocence is a filmy scarf
around her, rendering her and her baby pleasantly invisible. She
could ride this train almost indefinitely, at least for the 300 miles to
Kuwait. What she will do in Kuwait isn't clear yet. She has heard
how Western it is, the past and poverty, the righteous fierceness of
the religion, all covered over with oil money. Perhaps she will eat
Kentucky Fried Chicken there. She will buy a huge box of dispos-
able diapers. She will stay at the Kuwaiti Sheraton, take a hot
shower, sit on a disinfected toilet seat, sleep between soft sheets on
a mattress that never knew a flea, and decide whether to return to
Baghdad or Jerusalem or the United States.

They are at the outskirts of Baghdad now. A few passengers
debark, but more get on the train, pushing her to the back. She is
not particularly tired, just beginning to be hungry, when Ike starts
to cry. She looks at her watch. It is a while since he has eaten.
And he needs to be changed. Her heart starts to beat with almost-
panic. She can nurse him—in fact her breasts are starting to ache—
but she doesn't know the protocol, especially during Ramadan.
One of the other women is holding a baby, but older than hers;
earlier she'd watched him chew on an orange. Perhaps eating
during the day is permitted young Muslim children, just as Jewish
children are exempted from fasting on Yom Kippur. She could
nurse modestly if she were seated: Concealed by pleats in her
dress front are the appropriate slits. But standing in the aisle of
this crowded train she might inadvertently expose herself, an
accident for which the Koran, no doubt, decrees a large penalty.
She thinks of the two meters of fabric she bought, trampled on

the street now, or perhaps already scavenged, already cut and almost sewn into a long black skirt, an apron, a shroud? Ike's crying gets louder. Some people are looking at her, nibbling at her anonymity. She squeezes along the aisle in the hope of transferring cars, though she isn't sure she can transfer while the train is moving, or even if the doors open. Then at the far back of the car a man stands up from his seat. He's wearing a complete Western business suit, a gray matching jacket and pants. He is not wearing a *khafiyeh*. "Hello!" he calls out, pushing the man beside him over a little.

"I speak English!" she cries. "Do you speak English?"

"Such very good English," he says. "Please, Missus with the beautiful baby, please to sit down on this very fine seat. You are to Babylon going? To see the fabulous Hanging Gardens, yes?"

HE USED TO LIKE THIS, the something Wild West about her, but in their little apartment chock-full of objects she's taken a shine to, books she has started and not finished, it's making him mad, how she always chooses the path of greatest resistance.

There is a pattern. In Israel, where women serve in the army, she was a conscientious objector. Her first boyfriend was a Palestinian kid she called "my sweet lizard" and slept with (she'd said) on and off for a couple of years. She married a WASP, for God's sake, himself Winston Charles Wallace of Rosedale, St. Paul, Minnesota. She called herself a failed Israeli. But she has one thing in common with every Israeli he's ever met—she wears her personality on her hip like a six-gun.

Not even Jehovah was safe from her. There was a Bible story where God asked Abraham for the life of his only son. God backed off in the end and let Abraham sacrifice a ram, and probably He never wanted the human sacrifice in the first place; it was a test of Abraham's faith and love, that he passed with flying colors. But Dvora had talked about it as if it were her husband, her own Isaac. The idea of forcing Abraham to prove his love! What a paranoiac! (she really said that). Better Jesus Christ our Lord, a man-made God (her view), a cruci-fiction (her word), but at least He doesn't mess with your mind.

He turns on the ceiling fan, watches the blades pick up speed, rustling the pages of a book Dvora has left open. He thinks of their Isaac crying for his mother while she acts out her little tragicomedy. His anger is a fist pounding the back of his neck.

But understand, he tells himself. Dvora is smarter than you, has suffered more than you. Consider the messy, awful bundle of her loves and hates. Consider the effect of Muslim countries on the female ego. And the friend she lost to a bomb on a bus, a local bus on the way to a movie in Tel Aviv. After that, she told him, she wouldn't speak to her Palestinian friend or answer his letters. But she still loves him, he knows; she gets short of breath speaking of him. Thinking about it he digs his nails into the palms of his hands in order to stop thinking about it.

HE'S IN THE EXPORT BUSINESS: dates, en route to a meeting in Kuwait. English words roll around his mouth like dates. He looks at her with his full face as he talks, bathing her with his date-sweet breath. His name, he says, is John West.

"John West!" Her voice is shrill in her own ears. Still she can't calm herself. "This is not true?!"

He doesn't smile. His name is not a joke for them to share. But he doesn't mind the baby's legs on his lap as she changes him. He drapes her with his suitcoat so she can nurse in private. She says, "You are an angel of God."

"I, Missus, am a Christian."

She can't see him clearly on the dimly lit train but his whisper has the comaraderie of persecution shared. She allows herself a series of regular breaths. On this Arab train bound for a place she has never seen, John West is understandable. Not an Arab because not a Muslim (though she knows not all Arabs are Muslims). Perhaps an Arab but still a friend, cousin, a young uncle (he is perhaps forty years old), his religion so much less different from hers than either of theirs from that of their host country. "How is it," she asks, "to be a Christian in this Muslim land?"

"Wonderful, yessiree. Fabulous to be a Christian."

His smile is awkward, like a skill learned late in life, but presented, she feels, as a gift to her, along with the fact that he went to university in the United States of America. In the state of Texas, to be exact, the engineering school of the University of Texas, although, sadly, circumstances at home compelled him to leave before he could receive his degree. He speaks quietly but rapidly, with the accent of people from the American West, about his business, the climate, the Kurds, the increasing prosperity of Iraq only temporarily slowed by the war, the fabulous Hanging Gardens of Babylon, which she will be so pleased to see. Ike has gone back to sleep. She wants to sleep in the comfort of his pleasantly conveyed general information.

But she cannot sleep. Outside the window on top of a small rise stands another portrait of President Saddam Hussein, his full figure, boots to military cap, the plywood or whatever it was painted on, cut to his outline so that it casts a human shadow, more real for a moment than anything in the dim light of the train. John West, beside her, has moved from the Hanging Gardens to a description of Ur, where God first spoke to Abraham, and she sees Hussein's face before her, not cruel, just coarsely, powerfully whimsical, she wants to touch the dictator's close-shaven, fleshy cheek, the hard black hairs of his mustache. "A consecrated spot," says John West. "It holds much meaning in your religion."

"What is my religion?"

He whispers, "You are one-half Jewish."

She laughs harshly, clutching the remains of her secret of being a hundred percent Jewish, grandparents on both sides. "What else do you think you know about me? Where am I going?"

"To Kuwait. You have said, Missus, no?"

She cannot remember if she has said or not.

He goes on, "But you must not proceed all the way to Basra without stopping to see our fabulous national treasures of Iraq. The Hanging Gardens are perhaps not so beautiful as has been said, but Tall al-Muqqayar, ah! You must visit the Royal Tombs, and the remarkable Ziggurat, where the moon god Sin has been worshipped, best preserved of ziggurats in the world, in Ur of the Chaldees where all of our remarkable religions began; I would be a *chump* if I did not accompany you."

"I plan to meet with my husband," she says.

"In the city of Basra?" he asks.

"In the capital city of Kuwait."

"Very good, yessiree," he says. "From Basra you must to Abadan to buy your ticket to Al-Kuwait, which train, I know, will not depart until tomorrow in the morning. It is the train I am myself taking. Please, Missus. Ur is very near to Basra, the very shortest ride by bus or taxicab from Ur to Basra, very much wounded in the tragic war but quickly repairing, where is my own small and poor apartment at your service."

"I have too few diapers."

"In Basra are servants to wash for you. And still many beautiful hotels, with running water."

"Mr. West," she says, floundering for excuses though she is too proud for excuses. "My husband will be angry."

"He will have no reason to be angry," he says, extending both hands to her, palm up. "He will be pleased for you to be traveling under protection in this country, no longer in the midst of an unfortunate war, but still sometimes unkind to foreign women. He will thank Mr. John West for showing you to Ur and then to Basra where my servant will make for you delicious American food. Missus would like a tasty American burger?"

He smells not of dates but of sweet American aftershave, a gift, he says, from his American friend in Houston, Texas. He seems to have learned to speak from watching American cowboy movies, vocabulary, inflection. He is a sycophant, she thinks, an Americophile, for which she despises and then forgives him. To be a Christian among Muslims is like being a Jew among Arabs. She does not have to be afraid of him. She can feel perhaps superior to him.

"So it is agreed! Yessiree! You are hungry, Missus. Please to eat of my victuals."

He reaches down into the travel bag at his feet, takes out a small thermos, and opens it. The steam comes to her nose hot and strong.

"I have put much sugar," he says, "although I have more. Or perhaps first some treats from the market?"

He opens a paper bag, offers it. Dates and pistachios. She feels dizzy looking in the bag. Saliva fills her mouth. Her stomach squeezes.

"You are not hungry, missus?"

She swallows her saliva. Swallows again. She is very hungry. But in the act of taking his food is a contract she is signing; in Hades now she will not be allowed to leave. "We may not eat till sundown," she says, "while in Ramadan."

He laughs. "But you and I, Missus, we are not bound to the Five Pillars." He pours a cup of coffee. The train lurches. Coffee splashes her arm. "Missus," he says, "you must pardon our very poor trains of Iraq, rides most rough. If you will let me to assist you."

He sets the cup on the floor between his feet and holds out his arms for baby Ike. Her skin quivers where the coffee hit but there is no other sensation. The smell of the coffee makes her throat ache.

"Please, Missus," he says, "we must not drop this burning liquid upon his beautiful head. He is a boy, yes? A beautiful boy with such very white skin."

She puts her arms around Ike in his front pack, burying her nose in the fuzz on top of his head, but still she smells the coffee. Is coffee one of the exports of Iraq? Oil, dates, and coffee. She hands Ike to the man beside her. He holds him upright, under his arms, talking into his face. Ike makes a happy baby sound. John West seems gentler than Win, comfortable with children. She picks up the cup, orange plastic, as from a cheap lunchbox thermos. The coffee looks unutterably beautiful.

"Pardon me," he says, "but I see you are not liking my very good American Nescafé?"

It's hard to move her mouth even to talk. "I think they will throw stones at me."

"Nosiree," he says, pressing a couple of pistachios into a date and placing them in her half-open mouth. "While journeying even the followers of Mohammed may eat food during daylight hours." He bounces Ike up and down, supporting his head so it doesn't bob. "Do not be afraid. Allah is not so cruel as many people believe."

HE CALLS AN AMERICAN FRIEND from the embassy. He does not tell his friend that Dvora and Isaac have been gone, how many hours? He tells him what a hard time Dvora is having in Baghdad. And that he plans to wind up his business ASAP so they can go where the folks are blond and pale, where she can get into a good argument in a language she likes. Dvora looks beautiful arguing, he says into the phone, describing her flushed face, her rapid breath, her voice almost breaking in the excitement of making a point. Hanging up he feels as if the top of his head is coming off.

In the mirror his face is serene. He looks harder for signs of madness, an aimless flicker of the eye. Dvora's crazy mother has a slight wobble in her walk, as if she doesn't trust the continuing power of gravity. Dvora walks like her father, as if she owns the streets and sidewalks, as if she made them, as if her will as she walks is just now laying the curbs and crosswalks.

This is the personal style he most admires, he knows, based on the flashy wickedness of certain high school friends (most of whom have since succumbed to ordinary successes and failures, that still for some reason doesn't diminish their attractiveness). It has something to do with his response to Dvora. Right off he was a little overwhelmed by her; by her unswerving right steps, made right because of her belief in them. Other people felt it too, her fierce self-assurance, rock-hard, a little swaggering. When she talked, they listened; one of their college friends had confessed once to being afraid of her, of her lack of fear. As if (the friend had said this) she'd confronted something like paradox, an overwhelming thing that wouldn't resolve itself—she'd looked it in its multiple eyes and opened her arms. He thinks: Or not exactly opened them, but tried to and couldn't, couldn't but had to, kept on trying to, and so couldn't look away from the whole muddle of friends and enemies, terror and counterterror, her murdered friend and her sweet lizard, whom she wouldn't speak to but whose picture she kept, and all his letters.

He calls the operator, asks for the police. He misses Isaac. He is tired of thinking about Dvora.

THIS IS UR, NOW Tall al-Muqqayar, where God condensed himself out of His cloud and ordered Abraham to father His nation. She follows John West, though the tarred road burns through the soles of her sandals, though Ike's weight hurts her neck. She is thinking about Abraham, seventy-five and childless, to whom God said, Be fruitful and multiply. No fruit here now. A couple of small houses near the railway station. The land looks entirely barren, the color and topography of a brown paper bag, although, according to John West, four thousand years ago in the time of Abraham and Sarah, before the river changed its course, it grew rice and corn, dates and cotton, fertile and moist from the Euphrates.

"What made the river change course?" she calls out, unusual for her; she never asks questions. But she's a little dizzy in the heat, and her question is a link with the man who knows the way, whom she refused to let carry her baby. Her shoulders ache with the baby. Her purse hangs heavy from her arm. Her soles stick to the hot tar in the road, the thongs rub between her first and second toes, and she's so thirsty she has no saliva to swallow. This desert of asphalt and baked mud is hotter even than Baghdad, the heat deposited by the sun all day rising from the road to meet the heat still coming down from the late afternoon sun in what feels like a small, continuing explosion. The answer to her question shrivels into its separate words. At some point the road starts going uphill. At some point she passes through a gate in a chain-link fence, but she's too tired to pay attention. She has no energy to give to anything but how to avoid the puddles of melting tar on the road, so she is almost upon it before she sees the ziggurat.

But this is not possible. It's too tall, too large not to have insisted itself upon her long before her eyes rose to its height. It must have materialized there on these rocks, this baked mud, while she was picking her way through the pools of tar, as she stopped for breath, as if wanting something larger than life was for once powerful enough to create it, rising before her wider than it is tall but almost too tall to bear, an idol so big she can't imagine the force that can smash it. Thirty centuries haven't been able to smash it although they've erased everything else on all degrees of the horizon–nothing else taller than a shack here. Not even a shack, just the framework of what might have been a concession stand, now closed. She feels the impulse to kneel and lets it pass, not even rejecting it, hardly conscious of it, the yearning for gods or idols, older than Abraham.

"And this is only the first stage!" says John West as if he had something to do with it. "In the time of the Nabonidus, the last king of Babylon, it rose seven stages, seven terraces, over two hundred eighty feet of sunbaked brick, can one imagine?"

She shakes her head, though not at anything he said. She remembers the painting of the Iraqi president that she saw on the road to Babylon, now in her mind like a big paper doll. Up ahead what seems to be a staircase of enormous steps leads to the top of the ziggurat. On either side two other long ramps meet at the same point, though what is there she can barely see.

John West says, "On the seventh stage was built a shrine to Nanna, the moon god, that was father to the other gods, so these idolaters believe. His name it was also Suen, nickname Sin. That is amusing, yessiree!"

His cowboy accent clashes, she thinks, with his labored syntax. She walks away from him toward the foot of the nearest staircase. He follows.

"Notice the lines," he says. "They appear straight but in truth all curve inward, giving the eye the illusion of strength."

"Yes, of course." She puts her hand out and touches the bottom step. The risers are much higher than the treads are wide, as if the people who climbed them had long legs with tiny feet. With Ike dangling from her neck she begins to mount the ziggurat.

"Stop, please, Missus!" John West says. "It is not permitted!"

"There's nobody here!" she calls back.

"You will hurt yourself. The steps go very high!"

"I'm not afraid of heights!"

"It is a national treasure of Iraq!" he cries, pleading. She hears tears in his voice. "It is a desecration."

But the *shamal* has stopped, the wind that blocks up her pores and her ears with its sound. And the sun is low on the horizon, the angle of light turning the pale brick golden. Coolness in the air gives her new energy. "I am a Jew," she calls back. "I am Israeli-American, what is to desecrate?" She keeps on climbing, out of reach of anyone's judgment. The steps are so high she needs her hands to heft her up, and her feet hurt, especially between the first and second toes, and occasionally Ike's head grazes the edge of a step, but she climbs rapidly and fearlessly, since heights have never bothered her and desecration has no emotional content. "I am an atheist!" she calls out. "I am not a follower of Sin!"

She yells down from the top of the ziggurat, not expecting any response, just to hear her own strong voice. At the gate in the fence surrounding the ziggurat she sees two men in uniforms the color of the desert. One of them smiles and waves at her. A dog is barking in the distance, a familiar, almost friendly sound. But John West is climbing after her. She feels stinging now on the backs of her arms, not from bug bites but the sun. And her feet, she sees, are bleeding, have been bleeding a while, some of the blood already dried dark brown on the insole. There are bruises on two of her knuckles.

Do not wear sandals out of doors, she says to herself. Wear long sleeves.

THE POLICE ARE SEARCHING. They will call hospitals, hotels, train and bus stations, alerting officials throughout the city to a red-haired Western woman carrying a baby, easy to spot. He has heard the police of Baghdad are very good; efficient. He feels an almost idiotic relief.

These are the things he loves about Dvora: the way her features crowd together on her face, each demanding precedence. The way she calls him Mister America, not the name, which bothers him sometimes, but the way she says it, lingering over the *r*'s as if she's making fun of his language and liking it at the same time. How much she loves the United States of America, not the politics, of course, but the idea, and the feeling on the streets, as fervently patriotic as he at nine singing the national anthem so loud his throat hurt and writing letters to Johnson against people who burned the American flag.

He goes into the kitchenette, warms coffee, pours sugar with a heavy Middle Eastern hand. Dvora appears in his mind as a warrior in handcuffs wrestling a warrior without hands, both so brightly sunlit he can hardly see them. When the light subsides to what the eye can tolerate, she's standing by him at the sink trying to cool her bug bites with water from the tap. She gives him a look of scorn and pity. She tells him how she felt for a moment, in an adopted country, something like peace, a series of tranquil moments. In American cities with their scramble of clothing, speech, ways of seeing, no one had reason to stare at her so she could sometimes forget herself. Walking along American streets she didn't have to think about her Palestinian lizard and her murdered friend and her awful Jewishness. He sees: on the Baghdad streets she was visible again, an object of attention, if not hostility, for anyone with the leisure to look at her. Over dinner once their educated upper-class host, who hadn't dined with them, told them with a voice of passion that a woman was a man's most treasured possession. And gazing down at baby Ike in her arms, she knew she couldn't be his mother without being his Jewish mother, the means by which another Jew came to the fold, to be circumcised, bar mitzvahed, and taught he is both better and worse than everyone else in the world, that he both deserves, ineluctably, inalienably, his Eretz Yisrael, that he must inhabit it if he is to stay alive, only to see his Jewish-Israeli relatives—they're all relatives descended from Abraham—behaving so hideously to preserve it he feels hideous himself, till his sense of decency (which might, of course, be just the old Jewish "kick me," the sheep's obedient crawl to the ovens) says to the enemy, *OK, here, you take it if you want it so much.*

Is that puerile, Dvora Wallace née Blank? Is that amateur psychology?

THE LANDING WHERE the three stairways converge is rocky rubble with a few gray plants, the image, bounded and in miniature, of the ground below. The wind is utterly gone. The sun is gone too, vanished to red gold at the rim of the cloudless sky. Everything is cloudless, soundless, opaque blue, red, and gold, a bowl of sky so hard the slightest sound or movement will crack it open. She doesn't move. A few feet in front of her and slightly above the level where she is standing is a rock the size of a steamer trunk, the only protuberance on the expanse of rocky plain that forms the second level of the ziggurat. There is no shrine, no second flight of stairs, nowhere else to go. Someone is screaming.

The sound seems to come from somewhere below, and she wants to run. But there is nothing to be afraid of, not John West, a Christian, as kind and helpful as he could be. Nothing to fear but her own irrational fear and hatred of this man who calls himself John West, although an Arab. She stands motionless, looking at a single spot on the line where the sky and the ground meet, when her companion's head emerges over the rim of the stairs. She shrieks once, briefly. It's the first sound she has uttered herself, separating her from the awful noise, which comes—she looks where he is looking—from baby Ike in his pack. He says—sternly, she thinks—"He is angry, Missus!"

Ike is crying loud. His arms and legs are flailing, his head whipping back and forth. She turns her back on John West and touches her nipple to Ike's lower lip. The noise stops all at once, as if sucked back into where it came from. Ike smiles once, at the breast, then seems to collapse around it, sucking in hard, even tugs with his eyes closed.

"That is wonderful," says John West. "Yessiree. And do you know, up here it is very nice, such a very nice spectacular view!"

John West is looking at her as if she has performed a miracle. A kind look, warm and respectful. Ike is asleep in her arms, calm and rosy in the light from the setting sun. John West spreads out his sport coat in the shadow of the large rock, and she sets Ike upon it, stomach down. He continues to sleep. "It's an ordinary thing," she says. "Women do that." But she feels proud of herself.

"Yes, of course, that is true. Do you know, I believe that from here we can see to Basra!"

She walks over and stands slightly behind him. He seems younger than she'd thought at first; whatever lines she might have seen in his face are gone in the dying daylight. Right now he looks not much older than she. He is no taller than she. And inside his bulky business suit he is slim, much slimmer than her husband, frail, almost, like her lizard Ismal, Ismal with the long thin face, who hated Israel but not most individual Israelis, not *her,* she knew; who made her tea on the three-day march around Jerusalem, whose bedroom walls were papered with Donna Summers posters, whose wide ribcage and almost hairless chest she can still feel sometimes between her hands.

"It is so very beautiful here," says John West. "I believe that if we build restaurants and handsome Sheraton hotels we may entice many Americans here to see it. But we are in troubled times now, and this peace is so very weak and frail, we will not build handsome hotels."

She kisses him on the lips.

There is no give but no resistance. It's like kissing a tree.

She does it again, harder, opening his mouth with her tongue. He pushes her away, but gently. He probably has Prince on the walls of his Basra apartment, she thinks, Cher behind plexiglass. She can almost see the can of Nescafé in his cupboard, the bottle of American ketchup, and she feels tender toward him in a way she has never felt even with Ismal, tender and passionate enough to make love with him here on this desert island in the air while Isaac is sleeping.

But this is adultery, she knows, for which the Koran decrees death by stoning. She holds her breath for a moment, thinking of the Muslim punishment. In Pakistan it happened, deplored by lovely President Bhutto in her head scarf. But Win touches her so forcefully she has had to train herself not to flinch; it has been a long time since she wanted, really wanted, to make love with him. When the stones come for her she'll rise up in the air. Rocks will glance off her arms and the back of her head, touch her without harming. John West will touch her with questions in his small hands, the way a child touches a statue or an icon, something desirable and forbidden, forbidden because desirable, desirable because forbidden.

Ike starts to cry.

John West leaps away from her and kneels down beside the baby, who is crying louder than before, his back arching violently. Still she must forcibly pull herself out of what feels like a dream. She returns to the rock, takes the child in her arms, offers her breast again. The crying stops, he sucks enormously hard three or four times—then he throws back his head, opens his mouth wide enough to swallow the sky and roars, flailing in her arms like a fish.

Her head feels full, as if the bowl of sky has suddenly closed upon it. She is overwhelmed by something that translates itself into itching on her skin, not in any bounded scratchable spot but up her arms and her legs, toward the narrow passageways to the inside of her. She knows what is wrong. Her milk did not come down this time with the baby's sucking.

Cooing to Ike in her arms, she walks a circle around the flat rock at the top of the ziggurat. The heavy, dust-filled air makes her skin itch. She feels the tiny legs of Iraqi insects stepping through the tall grass of the hairs of her skin, insects so small they can crawl through mosquito netting, through openings in the weave of fabric, through her pores, she thinks, though she showered last night and this morning again with the prescription flea shampoo from the U.S. Embassy doctor. She hasn't slept in six months with the itching, with the wondering whether each sensation was a new bite or an old itch or a figment of her sensory imagination, and she is so tired now, it's hard to know what to do about what has just begun to come clear, that John West wants her baby. That's why he has brought her to this isolated spot, she is suddenly sure—to take her baby with his beautiful white skin, his mark of the sun on his temple. Her beautiful white American baby so much more valuable than a trainload of dates, a woman's most treasured possession. But this is a very crazy thought. John West is innocent and kind. She must guard against thoughts like this in this country so alien she can't look in anyone's eyes to see herself. Ike keeps on crying.

"Perhaps he is overheated." John West picks his jacket off the ground and starts fanning the baby with a sleeve.

"Take that rag away!" she says.

The baby keeps on crying.

"Perhaps a small date," says John West, reaching into his pocket.

"He does not eat solid food!"

"You may chew the date yourself, then deposit your saliva into his mouth, that is not uncommon."

[44]

She pretends not to have heard him. The baby keeps on crying.

"Perhaps he has received a bite or a sting. In this land are many harmful insects. If you please, to place him where we may inspect him." He spreads his jacket out over the flat rock. "Here, Missus. There is a slight declivity. He will not be able to roll."

The baby is bucking in her arms like a miniature wild horse. Even in the twilight she can see that his face is red. It gives off heat.

"Please, Missus." John West tries to take Ike out of her arms. She steps backward, holding Ike firmly. "I feel something," he says. "I believe there is a small bite. Shuh, little baby. Shuh, little boy baby."

The crying subsides somewhat. She allows John West to guide them over to the flat rock. He raises Ike's shirt, smiling with a squint of the eyes, a widening of the closed mouth. "Yessiree. It is becoming dark, Missus," he says, "but I have something from America that is very useful!" He digs in his pocket.

"What is that?"

"It will be all right."

In his hand is something long and slim that gleams in the dying light. Almost before she sees it she knows what it is. And knows it's a test. Of her faith and courage a test—that she will pass if she can place her son on the rock in front of John West. If she can open Ike's little blue shirt to the knife of John West, reciting the *Sh'ma* with her head bowed in obedience and faith: *Hear, oh Israel, the Lord our God, the Lord is One.* But she has no faith, sees no sense in obedience toward anything but her own desiring. Or maybe it's Ike's shriek stabbing her brain that makes her whirl the child away from John West just as he's pointing out with his tiny penlight, made in Dayton, Ohio, the small raised cap of an insect bite.

"Not poisonous, nosiree," he drawls, the line of smile widening his face, but knife or no knife, she sees beneath the smile and the business costume. He is an Arab, he is all Arabs, aflame with the righteousness of their cause inimical to her cause. Her body grows thick and strong, planting itself firmly on the crown of the ziggurat; it will not be pushed out of her country into any Mediterranean Sea. But he grows just as strong. They are equals in this place where their two nations were born. He is her one true husband.

The balance quivers a moment, precarious, lovely. Then her skin thinned by insect bites, or whatever sheath was keeping her parts together, begins to fray, to peel back, exposing to the dry air some raw terrified heart of her. She pulls her son off the altar of his sacrifice and runs for the stairway, the huge clay blocks of the stairs, the protection of the friendly guards, too fast to stop herself, her hands too full to grab onto anything, not that there is anything that can keep her from hurtling all the way down.

AT FIRST THERE WAS PEACE. It was as if, a moment before, a train had roared by. That's what he'd said to West, who'd seemed almost as shaken as he was; a fine person, West, the trouble he'd put himself to, bringing Ike back to Baghdad. There was peace. And there was Ike.

It remained true for a time even in this Israeli town of Herzliyya, even driving the multilane Israeli highway to Tel Aviv, where he will work for a while at simple sales distribution, not his old pioneering. It runs through his mind in Tel Aviv's rush hour traffic, in which he will spend a lot of time for the next few months.

In the evenings when the au pair is off he spoons bananas into Ike's mouth and burps and changes him, telling himself again and again: There is no one, nothing to blame but the ill-luck of birth and character and chance event, nothing anyone has control over.

But just when he thinks he has the story down—she was a victim of her psyche and her history, besieged from inside and outside, doomed to fight to her death like the state of Israel (tragic, but what could anyone do?)—and he'd work mindlessly hard all day and sleep all the way through, several nights in a row, like Ike down the hall, then he'll have a dream in which he is walking through the rooms of a huge house. He'll go farther and farther in, living room to bedroom to rooms off rooms, which get smaller till he can no longer stand up in them. And he'll wake with a scream he'll try to hide from the au pair, thinking about what West has told him about the country in which he lived a year without knowing. Its president, who smiled at babies in his portraits but decreed death for anyone who made him the butt of a joke—the law a joke, but on the books, said John West. Its mood of speechless terror, fear that cannot be voiced, what with informants at the bus stop, at the desk beside you, against not only Jews and Christians but good Muslim citizens, who naturally wouldn't confide to him, a foreign visitor, what they couldn't say even in front of their children. Children who might be tortured to make their parents speak. A baby Ike's age was deprived of milk, said John West, in the cell next to the cell where its father and mother sat hearing it scream.

On his good American double mattress in pretty little Herzliyya, named for Theodore Herzl, who'd fathered the Jewish component of the Middle Eastern horror, he turns from his back

to his stomach to his back again, knowing he missed it, the every-
day murk those people were choking on. And guilt comes, or
comes again, like a crab in the throat. In his two-bedroom apartment in this wealthy suburb of Tel Aviv (where there's a film studio, beautiful Jewish actresses; but why has he chosen to live
among Jews?) he thinks about what else he missed, what West
described to him, now so clear and bright before him in the night
his eyes water to see it—Dvora holding Ike in her arms as she fell.
What presence of mind, he says to himself. Heroic. Saintly,
maybe, the crab tightening its grip on the back of his throat. Then
Ike, whose random sounds have been getting luckier lately, flicks
his face with his starfish hand. "Aba ba ba ba ba," says Ike, and
then again, and then he stops at *abah,* Hebrew for father, fixing
him with his round baby eyes.

Next week when her parents visit (they come every Sunday,
her father silent beyond weeping, her mother tremulous with
presents for Isaac, carrier of the blood, the first grandchild and the
last) he will talk to them about Dvora. Because he didn't know her
as he might have.

And Ike will say "A da da da," and maybe "Ma ma ma," though
there is no Mama. And then, if they are lucky, *"abah,"* like a good
Israeli baby. And they'll clap for him and cry, "What a smart baby.
A brilliant baby!"

When they depart he'll hold Ike in his arms and rock and kiss
him and tell him he's a sweet, beloved, ordinary baby, no more or
less sacred than the lowest caste baby in the lowest caste country,
so that he won't plunder his enemy neighbors or plummet to an
early death. And later, as he sleeps, Win will whisper in his ear that

he's brilliant, blessed, chosen to save the world from the beasts and idiots who are ripping it apart. And hope he'll find his way past schizophrenia to a place where there is no contradiction.

Next year, writing his personal experience essay to convince admissions at Penn he's Ivy League material despite uneven grades, he'll describe in amusing detail the one baseball game his father took him to, and get in on a scholarship despite his father's explicit pessimism. And he'll do well although he's not as brilliant as his father, just a pretty smart kid who's used to working hard. But now on Rachel's bed, unraveling a hole in the knee of her jeans while her parents yell at each other downstairs, he cannot join in her raillery. "Let's go," he says.

"Wait, Demian! This is the part about who was the first unfaithful one!"

"Let's go!" he says. He has a curfew, a job to get up for tomorrow. Then there's the air outside the house, the smell of new grass mixing with the smell of Rachel when she lets him touch her under her T-shirt.

"Deem, listen! It's funny, really. It's high comedy."

From downstairs comes the froth of slurred bluster, followed by the sound of a chair scraping the floor.

Demian feels his ears shut down, the aural counterpart to the half squinting he does in the gory parts of horror movies. Rachel likes horror movies. She doesn't protest, however, as he takes her hand and leads her down and outside. He escorts her gingerly, like a boy walking a leopard.

Rachel is seventeen, a year older than he is, though in the same grade. She lost a year when she went, as she said, looney, and spent several months in the bin getting her spirit broken to the point where she'd attend school and respond, numbly, to teacher and test questions. Still her grades are better than his. Sometimes it seems to him he can't stand her, half an inch taller than he is, the way when she's not thinking about it she arcs down into herself like a long-necked bird, the way tall girls aren't supposed to. He used to love to play baseball, it was all he wanted to do—if not on the field, then in a symbolic version with cards and dice in his room—and when this feeling of loathing comes over him it brings on a desire for base-ball, for playing shortstop, to be specific, standing between second and third with his knees bent, whispering in the direction of the bat-ter—hit it to me, I dare you. He remembers his two best friends from then, brothers a year apart, Tom and John Frank, the clean, sharp edge of the way they bad-mouthed each other after the game. And then the queasiness comes, because something he has done with Rachel or is about to do has rendered him unfit for baseball.

He walks quickly now, a step ahead of her, over to the play-ground behind the local preschool, where they've gone the past months to talk and kiss and perform all but the final technical act of sexual intercourse. The ground is laid in gravel through which hard weeds poke up, but the chain-link fence is low enough to climb over, the large wooden sandbox lies half in the shadow of the building, the sand is cool and dry and molds after a while to one or the other's back.

Tonight, though, they do not embrace. Rachel sits down on the dark side of the sandbox. At first she seems to have disappeared. Then he sees in the dark the lesser darkness of her face, the pale stretch of her shoulders, too wide for a girl. She smells sour and sweet like strawberries. He is suddenly moved by something in Rachel, her craziness, her cynicism, facets of personality he dimly perceives he may have to own some day. He remembers an assembly where she danced in center stage with the other dancers weaving around her, her turns and leaps bolder than theirs, more complete. "Rachel," he says, "I really like you."

She doesn't respond, but the slight prickle of the skin of his arms tells him he has said the wrong thing. He tries again. "You're a really good dancer." He compares her dancing to the way he used to feel about baseball. Still feels sometimes. She doesn't help him out. Her silence is a hole he walks around and around.

"Rachel," he says in despair, "I feel bad for you. How you survive so well with—"

But he doesn't want to talk about her parents. Their dads by some fluke knew each other in college, and Rachel's sometimes asks him how his father's doing, a show of interest or courtesy his father doesn't return. Demian himself can barely manage to speak to her father, who makes more money than his father and calls him the Old Hippie. "Ask him about Woodstock," Mr. Geller once said, and Demian said, "Why don't you ask him yourself," knowing his father hadn't gone to Woodstock, as Mr. Geller also knew. Mr.

[55]

Geller is soft-looking and bottom heavy like an old pear. Demian can't stand Mr. Geller, has only broached the subject of her parents as a gift for Rachel.

She says, "They're not my real parents."

He laughs, though she has said that before.

"I'm going to divorce them," she says. "There's a new law, in Vermont."

"Massachusetts, I think."

She shrugs, irritated with his quibble. He talks quickly to assuage her. "Then you can marry *my* parents."

"Who wants your parents?"

"What's wrong with my parents?"

"Your father has a mean streak."

"No, he doesn't!"

He is suddenly aware that his eyes have adjusted to the light. He can see the parts of her face that jut out, eyebrows, cheekbones, slope of nose. She seems too sharply constructed, a witch-woman, though she's sitting cross-legged like a child, pouring handfuls of dry sand over her thighs. "He won't let you do stuff for no reason," she says. "For spite."

Demian knows that in similar words he has complained to her about his father, who gave him a curfew earlier than most of his friends' younger brothers, frequently refused him permission to attend parties, and who wasn't planning–he'd warned him–to let him get his driver's license till he was eighteen years old. Teenagers have glop for brains, he'd said. Though as a teenager himself–his mother had told him–he'd dropped out of college and done a lot of the drugs teenagers were supposed to say no to these days. Demian hasn't really spoken to his father since the day he refused to sign the learner's permit. But now Demian says, "He has his own ideas. He does what he thinks is right and not what everybody else does!"

She claps her hands.

"What is that supposed to mean?"

"You are so *canned!*"

He's about to stand up, leave, maybe, something to punish her disrespect for his father and himself. But she takes his arm. "Demian, I love you."

"So you can say anything you want to me?"

She puts her arms around him, thrusts her tongue into his mouth. He keeps up his end of the sexual bargain. Soon he is urgent, panting. She, too. His fingers are wet with her. As usual at this point he tries to pull off her shorts. As usual she pushes away from him. Once he questioned her, learned that her noncompliance had to do, not with some gap or lack in his feeling for her, but with something apologetic she detected in his attitude toward sex. Since then his protests have been mild, ritualized. She is his first real girlfriend. He is pleased to be kissing and touching her even at the level of intimacy she has ordained. She hurls herself at his hand, trembling.

HE HAS TO BE HOME BY 10:30 and it's 11:35 by the oven clock as he tiptoes across the kitchen. He has never missed curfew before, but the evening is still warm on his skin; he feels invulnerable. And his father is surely asleep.

He takes his shoes off in the living room. His father is *inactive*, his mother says. Understatement of the year, Demian thinks. Tired from working in the bookstore, which doesn't bring in enough for him to hire a manager, his father often falls asleep on the couch in front of the ten o'clock news, and Demian and his mother have to prod him up to bed.

But he's up now, standing in his pj's at the top of the stairs. His long, thin, still young-looking face is blank; not even his lips seem to move as he says, "You're grounded." His lips are pressed close together, a tuck in the long swatch of his face, but the words linger in the air well after his lanky body has turned and vanished behind the master bedroom door.

In bed Demian is stiff with fury. There is no recourse; the only question is how long. And even worse than not seeing Rachel is seeing her with the weight of his father's edict on his shoulders, bowing them, making him smaller than he is, unworthy of her.

Four years from now Demian will fly home from college to watch his father breathe in comatose sleep, then cease breathing, and Demian will go numb, because from now on nothing he does for good or ill will have any impact on his father. Later in his mind he'll rage at his father for dying before he, Demian, was ready for him to die, and later still he may decide that if his father wasn't ideal he did the best he could. But now Demian has hopes for what he can be to his father and what his father can be to him, and he dreams his father on the eighteenth floor of a burning building and he, Demian, running up flight after flight of stairs to save him.

DEMIAN IS UP HOURS BEFORE he has to leave for Bi-Rite's, rehearsing the speech he will give his father at the breakfast table.

He's got it outlined in his head like a five-paragraph essay, and now with the sun turning the sky pink, then blue, he sits at the kitchen table while his mother, who has to leave soon to teach summer school, performs five or six brisk cleaning and cooking acts. His father sips coffee. His father butters a piece of rye toast, as slowly as an old man, though his hair is still thick, his face unlined; people sometimes think he's Demian's older brother. Demian says casually into the space between bites, "I want you to reconsider."

His father looks to the left, the right, all around the room. "Who's talking? Is somebody talking to me?"

Demian's ears feel hot. This is the first direct statement he's made to his father in several months. "Dad, I'm never late. I shouldn't be punished the first time I mess up. Give me a second chance."

"Look, you." His father's voice is papery quiet but it seeps into every corner of the room. "If some dude walks into my store with a gun, and I say, hey now just wait a minute, do I get a second chance?"

Demian thinks he sees some illogic in his father's argument but his father stands up, leaning forward as if about to fall on him. "If you get sick, Kiddo, if your heart hurts, air sticks in your throat, you say with your last feeble breath, God, Jesus, Krishna, whoever—please, what did I do, could you please, please give me a second chance, what's He going to say to you? Tell me, Demian."

Demian wants to ask his father what makes him think he's God, but the molecules of air in the room are moving too fast to let in any more words.

"Let's say you get your girlfriend pregnant, Demian. Let's say for the sake of argument you knock up your young lady. But you aren't ready to be Papa yet. You want to walk across Turkey in your stocking feet. You want to climb Mount Tamalpais and keep on going."

His father has just said more to Demian, it seems, than he's ever said before in his life. His hands are waving, his face is white. Demian's mother pats his back, leads him back to the table. Though she's running late, she gets him more coffee, hovers over him, till his face warms up. He kisses her good-bye a beat longer than he has to. Says nothing to Demian. Demian feels sick, choking on the words he can't speak to his father. "Mom," he whispers after the door is shut, "is he mean, or what?"

"Demian," she says, "you've got to give him some slack. The business isn't going well."

"Who cares?" Demian's voice rises. Every once in a while he's allowed to sneer in front of his mother. It's his one respite, acting like his father in front of his mother. "Mine isn't going well either." He watches her face, prepared to shut down at the first sign of her disapproval.

"Demian," she says, "he may have to declare bankruptcy. Don't say anything to him, please. Eat your breakfast."

Her lips look blue, like the lips of little kids who have been in the water too long. Demian eats his cereal, a piece of toast, then, absentmindedly, the rest of his father's toast. It's not even eight o'clock, he has plenty of time. He eats while his mother says nice things about his father. How good he is to her. How well his friends like him, even the rich, much-respected ones. Demian is aware that people listen when he speaks. Demian would like his own friends to treat him as his father's friends treat his father. Sometimes he quiets his voice, thins it out a little, to see if that's the trick. "He's way too smart for what he does," his mother says, her pale blue eyes burning into his forehead with the truth of her message. "He did well in college without studying. He could remember everything he'd ever read. He was a great talker, there was nothing he couldn't have done if he'd wanted to, do you know how high his IQ is?"

"Higher than mine," Demian says.

His mother doesn't protest, just shakes her head as if in wonder. "He never got time to sit and figure things out. He was too young to have a child."

"Mom," Demian says, "he was twenty-six when I was born. He's forty-two."

"He was too young," she says firmly, gathering up her books. "But he loves you like crazy, you ought to know that."

PEDALING TO WORK Demian thinks about his father's IQ, how many points it might be higher than his own, and tries to see him as the Disappointed Man in his mother's fiction. He says "bankrupt," under his breath, trying to diminish his father enough to forgive him. It doesn't work. He tries to feel his father's love for him, remembering a ballgame his father took him to on his tenth birthday—him and his best friend John Frank and John Frank's father. He remembers sitting next to John in the back of their old Rabbit with his baseball glove in his lap for catching foul balls. Remembers listening to his father up front talking with John's father, John's father laughing at his father's jokes though John's father drove a Volvo and people called him Dr. Frank. Demian was proud of his father. It was clear even then that although his father talked less than his friend's father it was his father's words that stayed in the air of the car, hovering around their heads like cigar smoke. His father had given him and John their own tickets to hold, and jouncing along on the backseat they squinted at the blue and white cardboard oblongs, discussing the numbers and letters that stood for what they were about to experience. SAT AUG 6 1:20 PM. AISLE 518 ROW 5 SEAT 242. GAME #52 CHICAGO CUBS –vs– NEW YORK METS. ADMIT ONE SUBJECT TO CONDITIONS ON BACK NO REFUND NO EXCHANGE. There was one set of letters he couldn't fathom: OBST VW. He showed the ticket to John. "Obstetrician?" John asked.

"It's a beer ad. Obst Blue Ribbon!"

"That's *Pabst* Blue Ribbon."

"I know, fart-head!"

Only when they got to the park and sat down in seats behind a pillar that let him see half the field if he craned to the right did he realize the letters stood for *Obstructed View*. At first he didn't mind. He'd never been to a major league game before. The smell of hot dogs and popcorn filled his mouth and nose, the stands were cool and dim like a naptime bedroom, the playing field so bright green under the sun made his eyes water. He put his glove on, waiting for his father to sit down next to him, not necessarily to talk to him, since of course he had more to say to Dr. Frank, but just to be there so Demian could ask him questions or maybe just sit quietly beside him, watching him watch the game. But when Demian had finished taking in the mix of brightness and darkness, and located his favorite

Cub, Shawon Dunston, who could hurl the ball like the end of a whip, his father was still standing in the aisle. "We'll get you guys after the game," he called to them, holding out a five-dollar bill. "Don't eat too much." Demian took the bill, folded and folded it again as his father and Dr. Frank descended the precipitously steep steps, vanishing toward seats Demian knew had an unencumbered view of the field. Still he wasn't sure what to make of the turnaround. It wasn't exactly what he'd pictured when he'd asked on his tenth, his double-digit birthday, not for something to ride or look at or hold in his hand but for an event to experience with his father. The man who took his father's seat told him stories about the ball players' personal lives. It was lots of fun sitting with John, leaning hard one way around the pillar to watch the ball come off the bat, then the other way to see where the ball ended up. Shawon Dunston threw the ball into the dugout, and the Cubs still won. But although he and John wore their gloves all nine innings the foul balls all went to seats below them in the sun. And although they kept good track of the game, marking the P.O.'s, F.O.'s, K's, H's on their scorecards with their short yellow ballpark pencils, some of the balls fell where neither of them could see them. The man in his father's seat said Shawon Dunston would never learn to take a walk because he was mentally retarded. When Demian's father returned for them after the game the skin of his arms looked dark gold in the sun, and Demian was sure that the game he'd seen was not as good a game.

DEMIAN LEANS BACK in his chair at the Geller breakfast table, puts his feet on a second chair, takes the cup of coffee Rachel has poured him. He's never had coffee before and he gulps it like milk, burns his throat, swallows his grimace. Rachel doesn't ask him why he isn't at Bi-Rite's this morning, and he doesn't explain. She talks rapidly, of nothing he has to respond to; he tries to rest in the quick-woven shelter of her voice. She's barefoot, in a long, wrinkled shirt she must have slept in. He imagines further what's under the shirt. His face burns. Her brown hair looks white blond on the side where the sun hits. If he were to speak he thinks his voice would mewl like a scruffy cat.

She runs into the kitchen, returns with kiwi and nectarines on a dark blue glass plate, and two blue cloth napkins. But on the pale gray tile of the kitchen floor she has left patches of red. She is limping. He watches, frozen, as blood wells out of her foot. She sits down, crosses her leg over her knee, eats a nectarine, while her blood drip-drips onto the gray tile. He thinks, Why doesn't she wipe it up? Should he wipe it up? Someone should wipe it up. It gives him the creeps, these bright red splashes, but the cloth napkin seems too fine for this use. He's looking around for paper when she throws a piece of broken china onto the table in front of him. "Parental carnage," she says.

It's the source of her injury, picked up from the kitchen floor— a white shard, triangular in shape, a thin gold line around the part that had been rim. The broken edge is red with her blood. "Car*nage,*" she says, accenting and softening the last syllable like a French word. This morning her father had relieved some of his anger by throwing a cup at the refrigerator. Her mother relieved hers by refusing to sweep. "They need to *see* this!" she says, placing the broken piece of china on the blue cloth napkin in the middle of the breakfast table. She seems thrilled almost, as if the bloody shard is the final piece of the jigsaw puzzle of her life. She arranges a kiwi on the napkin, a bud vase alongside. "It's our new center-piece! A still life! What'll we call it, *Terror at Teatime?*" She speaks with a British accent, biting off her words with her teeth. "No, something simple: *Daddy!*"

He starts laughing, at first quietly, then with gusto. "That's terrific," he says. "It's really funny." He laughs in loud, discrete bursts, like a train tooting. He has never laughed like this before. He tells her the story of the one baseball game his father took him to, exaggerating his hopes so that their obstruction by the pillar seems purely comic. She takes his hand, squeezing hard, and he elaborates, this time stressing his naïve reverence for his father, his father's indifference. What had his father called out, descending the stairs? Demian doesn't remember now, makes it up: "Look, you–you're lucky you weren't offed in utero." It doesn't sound like his father but makes him laugh hysterically.

She starts laughing too. "He slapped me this morning. I told him what I thought of people who couldn't control themselves and he slapped my face. Twice. Once on each side. For symmetry." She puts her hands flat to her two cheeks, opens her mouth like the man in *The Scream.* "He said, 'Is this self-control? Tell me, if you're so brilliant?'"

He moves his chair nearer to hers. He's trembling, though he doesn't feel sad or scared. "Sometimes in the room with him I feel like I don't exist. I don't have a body. I don't know how to talk, even." He's shaking down to the soles of his feet. He has never spoken words like this. "He'd slap me, too, if he thought I was important enough. The truth is, I bore him. Poor Dad, bored by his son." He replays what he said, awed by what seems to be the utter truth of it. It seems reckless and marvelous saying these things about his father. He's an explorer, charting ground never before seen by mortal eyes. "I really don't need him. If he died tomorrow it wouldn't make the least difference in my life. It might improve things."

Years later, with his father's vein leaking into his brain, he'll remember what he said to Rachel now, and even though over the years his father had grown no more interested in him, he'll think for a moment of all the things his father wanted to do that he couldn't do, couldn't now ever do, and he'll sit down in a chair by the bed, for a moment unable to breathe. But now he's on his knees before Rachel's chair. She puts her arms around his shoulders, presses her face to the top of his head. He hears her heart beating through her T-shirt. His teeth are chattering, and to stop them he starts kissing her through her shirt–her shoulder, the two round little bones at the top of her chest, the long swell of breast. In the past he has treated this part of her body reverently, but now he sucks as if he were drinking, wetting the cloth of her shirt till it feels to his lips like rough, wet skin. He has stopped trembling. "I hate him," he murmurs, almost lovingly.

"Has he ever knocked your mother down? Called her a slut? Said he could smell it on her? I'm in the same room, here at this very table eating my cantaloupe."

He can't tell if she likes what his mouth is doing, but she has made no objection. He raises her shirt, observes her body in the daylight; thinks, *There is so much of her.* He says, "He made me sit behind a pole. He traded in his ticket and sat with a buddy. The only baseball game he ever took me to."

It doesn't sound quite awful enough. He looks at her for confirmation, but she seems not to have heard him. She says, "Has he ever come home drunk and gotten in bed with you? And when you screamed he put his hand over your mouth? And when you bit his hand he told lies to your mother? Who still thinks you're a slut though she doesn't say so?"

"Is that true, Rachel?"

She shakes her head no. "Another example of my sick imagination."

Her voice is light but he can't shake off the terrible picture. "If it were true I'd kill him."

"Me, too."

Her last comment came without inflection. He tries to read her face but it doesn't help. He hugs her hard; she returns it with a slight time lag, mechanically stroking the back of his head. She seems uncharacteristically passive. He feels sure that if he were to take off his pants she'd sigh once, then render her body penetrable. The thought terrifies him. "Rachel, where are you?"

She looks at him, smiling with the corners of her mouth only. He wants to be gone from here, to be riding back to Bi-Rite's, whose manager is a friend of his dad's and might not question the excuse he'll make up on the way. But Rachel is sitting so still in her chair she seems to take up no space. If he left, he thinks, he'd never find her again. When he called, her mother would say, *She's traveling in Europe.* Her mother would say, *There's no one here by that name.*

"Rachel," he whispers. He touches her face, the curve of her arm, side of her knee, arch of her wounded foot, softly so as not to miss her faintest whispered response. Her foot feels cold, and he warms it between his hand and his face. Then, starting from the beginning he puts his lips to the injured spot, licking off the dried blood with his tongue, smoothing down the flap of torn skin.

❦ Small Talk ❦

Daniel is sick. Daniel Steinman, my first cousin, a musical genius (says the family and the *Plain Dealer;* not yet *The New York Times*). Steinman, twenty-seven, current musical director of *The Fantasticks,* New York's longest running play, is sick, maybe dying. Is this what we all think?

"He should never have moved away from Cleveland," says Auntie Mildred, my mother's oldest sister. Mildred, my childless aunt, the only sane one (my father would insist) besides my mother. Mildred, who visits New York often for the musical theater. She and Uncle Am took Daniel to see *Evita* last month and then out to eat in Chinatown where he kept running to the bathroom. In Cleveland Heights now, at her own dinner table, lengthened for my holiday visit, Mildred expands on her concern for Daniel—in the middle of courses, setting down his chopsticks, excusing himself. His face looked awfully thin. And Thanksgiving, she says, what is he doing with himself tonight, Thanksgiving?

Aunt Mildred's face is square and smooth, younger than her sixty years, though now creased with disapproval of what is going on this holiday away from us. "I made him promise to see a doctor," she says to Celie, Daniel's mother, who is enormously fat and always looks cold. Arthur, Daniel's father, shakes his head. "Daniel has always had a nervous stomach. Daniel is a very high-strung individual."

They turn to me, Daniel's contemporary, for a confirmation, but I do not comply. My mother fills in: "Mimi used to call him 'intense,' isn't that the word, sweetie?" Aunt Mildred nods emphatically. Aunt Celie looks blank for a moment, then says something blithe, unsyntactical, and not quite to the point. She met Arthur when he was a soldier in Europe during the Second World War, so she has lived here more than forty years, but her conversation is still hard to follow–not because of her accent, as my mother thinks, but because it's never to the point, as if it's meant to convey only the effect of conversation. My grandmother, called Bubby, who, though eighty-two and blind, is devoted to "Sixty Minutes", who in the last presidential election walked three blocks in her walker to cast her vote, whose long German vowels and hissing consonants make it hard not to grasp what she says, declares, "It's that new disease."

Silence rises up from somewhere in the middle of the table, a dense little ball, swelling this way.

"I like to eat the Chinese," says Aunt Celie. "The oil of Chinese is light, you do not become fat." Her voice spirals up into the beginning of a giggle.

Later my mother will take my face in her hands, looking to the back of my eyes like a doctor for some disease of blindness. "You're too thin," she'll say, and I'll say, "Thank you, Mama."

Still later, flying home to Chicago I see Daniel sick: Every time he thinks he is better at last (I imagine) the pain returns, the cramps, the spasmodic flow that one night he won't be able to stem.

BUT DANIEL IS NOT SICK. Uncle Arthur took him to Israel, to that country with more doctors per patient than any other country in the world, this one included, and he received a "clean bill of health." Daniel is well; fine. In the spring now, here at my mother's Seder table we see for ourselves. He's not thin but lean; he has always been lean. We look at him approvingly, the lean, determined planes of his cheeks. Arthur puts an arm around him. Daniel has quit his job with *The Fantasticks*, he says. Daniel is back with them for a time, in the clean, comfortable house he grew up in, in the bed he used to sleep in, which is just what he needs now: continuity. Arthur believes in continuity, pursuing the subject as if it will extend time for us indefinitely, as if it's a synonym for immortality. "I make for him food," Celie says. "Breakfast, lunch, dinner food." They speak loudly, not looking at Daniel, their only child, sitting between them with a pleasant expression on his face. "Soft cooking eggs," Celie says.

Daniel, clearly, is laboring to do his best for us. His eyes move from speaker to speaker. He smiles, if not at a joke's punch line, then just a beat later. In those gaps in the flow of time when the conversation bumps into itself and stops for a second, his gaze drops to the Haggadah and his mouth starts to move, perhaps practicing his part in the Seder where, as the youngest child present, he will ask the Four Questions. "Daniel," I whisper, "welcome to Fantasyland."

[*B*]

"Thank you," he says, as if I'm one of the aunts.

At dinner in sweet and fluent Hebrew he sings the Four *Kashehs* but asks no other questions. Ours he answers briefly. No, he has not given up his New York apartment. No, he hasn't composed much since the musical director job—no time, or no something; yes, it's a shame. No, he will not entertain us at my mother's piano, but thank you for asking. He thanks my mother for the wine she pours into his glass but he doesn't drink it. "I'm sure you'll start something new," says Mildred, "now that you're home?" I look him in the eye but see nothing there to stop me; I fall and fall.

After dinner I catch Uncle Arthur in a corner of the room and I ask, "How *is* he?"

"How does he seem?" says Uncle Arthur. He has a sort of beam on his face, as if he's about to show me the stock market page, the closing price of the family business which he has run since my grandfather died.

"Like a zombie," I say.

Arthur, who always acts as if we have a special connection, takes my arm and pulls me into my old bedroom, now the sewing room. "He had a nervous breakdown," he says, squeezing my arm as if to reassure me. He gives me a wet kiss on the cheek. Something pricks my stockinged heel, a pin in the long shag of my mother's rug. He is gone before I can ask my next question.

IN THIS FAMILY (Steinman—stone men—masons, it was thought) we do not transmit or absorb information. Our mental walls are thick and rock-hard. Or we are stone-deaf.

But there is adultery here (I believe). An illegal abortion. An early death that may be suicide. I didn't know my father was dying of cancer (it was called a "spot on the lung") until I came home from college one spring, and he fell getting out of bed, and my mother started crying. Maybe the pact is that information is not to pass cross-generationally. There is no one in the room—not even Bubby, whose pronouncements do not thin out into conversation—who might discuss with me the fact that Daniel is gay.

Although Daniel told me himself. "I've discovered something," he said to me nine or ten years ago, age seventeen maybe, already known in Cleveland for his piano-playing, the score he'd written for a local musical comedy. I was reading on a chaise longue on Bubby's porch. I put my book down and moved my feet for him. "It's about me," he said, "but it might interest you."

Interest me? I was flattered. I was at the time the last person I'd have chosen to receive a confidence—a blatant impostor, newly back from India unenlightened and soon to be divorced, at twenty-four too old to be credible based on potential alone—on, for example, my little Super 8 film about a Heights High School AFS student, judged second in the state of Ohio in high school filmmaking, an achievement that at twenty-four I hadn't improved on, but that's another story. In this one I'm reading on Bubby's huge, cool, dim front porch with the tile floor and the brick columns, away from the after-dinner relatives who used to sit over Sanka pondering which of my multiple talents would bear fruit, who are now saying, "Well, at least there weren't children." Aunt Helen is alive now at the end of the dining room table, my mother's favorite sister, tiny and sweet-voiced, indulgent with her two wild boys, still in love—you

ee it—with her handsome husband. My divorced twin aunts,
e and Loretta, one of whom works frighteningly hard for a
living and the other not at all, have flown in from Boca Raton trailing the sad stories of their lives: Louise's infant daughter who died
of polio, Loretta's obese gangster son who hasn't spoken to her
since the divorce when he chose to live with the father, and who
once, incidentally, rubbed his thick hand over my new-grown
breasts, an invasion I never told anyone about and for which I will
never forgive him, but that's another story. In this one my mother
and her four sisters pincer up saccharine pills from a tiny brass dish
on the dining room table, their opinions spilling out to me through
the front screen door on my choice of a husband, a line of work.
Which I endure knowing I'll be in Chicago soon, 350 miles away
from all this expectation and disappointment. In four or five years
Daniel too will stretch the cord that ties him to Cleveland, farther
than I have, in the other direction. In the meantime he seats himself on the courteous far end of my lounge chair and after a question or two about my ex-husband, whom he'd admired, and my
ex-guru, whose book he'd bought, tells me about the boy he's in
love with. Who loves him back. Eyes shining with the daring/new-
ness of it all.

I would like to remember what I said. I remember what I was
reading, *Psychotherapy East & West*. But everything I think to say
now—It's great you know that, Daniel—it takes courage—I have
those feelings too—sounds unctuous or goofy and I was in no shape
to do better then.

I do remember his long oily hair of a high school hippie, his
long-fingered hands with their nails chewed down, the tips inflamed

pink, an occasional drop of blood where nail should have been. Bloody fingertips, but good for playing the piano–nothing to click on the keys, distract the artist from his art. Nothing to discompose, to prevent from composing. In those fingers so exposed, so fearless in the expression of themselves there was something to be loved. And if I didn't love him, I at least loved the way I felt talking with him, my homosexual young genius cousin, a quarter of whose blood–I'd worked it out–was from the same place as a quarter of mine.

But this is false. I felt heterosexual desire for him, so remote from me behind all the big and little taboos. When the family massed onto the porch we stayed on our island of a lounge chair. We listened snickeringly, passing ironic looks back and forth when an aunt or cousin said something foolish or typical.

DANIEL IS IN THE HOSPITAL. The phone doesn't ring in his room. No one is supposed to see him. This is what my mother says Aunt Celie said. He's too sick, stuck with tubes, a respirator. He doesn't want visitors. He can't speak, can't recognize people.

It's a tragedy, my mother reports on the long-distance phone, earnestly, unequivocally, like a newscaster. I'm suspicious. "He doesn't want visitors or he can't recognize them? Which?" I say.

"I don't know. Either. Both."

"It can't be both!"

"Miriam, don't raise your voice to me."

I yell in a whisper. I want her to hate Aunt Celie, who has raised this fog of confusion and terror around Daniel. She's the troll on the bridge, the sleepless dog at the Gates of Hell. "How can you believe anything she says? You know she's crazy!" It's true. Even when Daniel was young and their family more or less trouble-free, she wore long-sleeved sweaters in hot summer and hid boxes of chocolates in secret places all over the house—bathroom drawers, the piano bench—and couldn't make small talk without a hysterical giggle.

"She grew up in a foreign country."

"So did Bubby."

"She's his mother," my mother says.

"Mom, he's dying too fast! I've read stuff on AIDS. There are gays where I work. One of them looked like a *ghoul,* sores all over his face, but now he's back waiting on tables, he seems perfectly healthy!"

"Mimi," my mother says, "you've got to stop this."

QUESTIONS I CAN'T ASK:

(1) What did Aunt Loretta do to her loathsome son to make him hate her?

(2) Why did Aunt Helen, my mother's youngest and prettiest sister, die before the age of forty?

(3) Why did her husband marry so soon afterward (Gloria, a shiksa, his dental hygienist)?

(4) Why did Celie wait twelve years before getting pregnant with Daniel?

(5) Why won't anyone admit that Celie is crazy?

(6) What made my grandparents, so brilliant and vital, with their six children living into adulthood and their business grown from a hardware store into a corporation on the stock exchange (American), produce a family that will, barring a miracle, die out after this generation? (The Steinmans, Stonemen, worn to gravel?)

(7) How is Daniel really?

THERE ARE ALLEGED ANSWERS, but as bald and vague as press releases. Aunt Celie, of course, had a series of "misses." Aunt Loretta had a fiend of a husband who stole from Grandpa's business and turned their son against common decency. Aunt Helen had a tumor, which grew like a baby inside her skull—my mother's closest sister whom we used to vacation with—and the real tragedy is the boys, lost to the West Coast and their stepmother, California surf and drugs, we never hear from them....

I'm thirty-three years old and I have a job that pays for my rent and occasional vacations, and if my mother God forbid should die and leave me penniless I'd still manage to support myself without government or family aid, unlike Aunt Loretta who lives by sole means of Grandpa's estate, and I suspect that on the inside of one of Celie's wrists are the numerals of a concentration camp survivor, but I am told nothing.

Not even (8) why I, so early-brilliant with my teenage awards and my B.F.A. (film), live now an almost wholly imaginary life, working as a waitress (albeit a competent and respected one in a cloth tablecloth restaurant), writing treatments in my mind for a few minutes in bed at night before I fall asleep.

AUNT CELIE DISAPPEARS. Along with a small suitcase and—fodder for much discussion—her bathroom scale. Arthur, Mildred, my mother, all are frantic. A week later she turns up at the Sheraton in downtown Cleveland. Is found alive in a room at the Sheraton. And well, everybody says. After checking in under the blatantly gentile name of Christina Kent she apparently sat down on the bed in her room and turned on the television, moving to the chair when the maid came to clean and then back to the bed again. As far as the management knew she stayed in her room the entire week. She didn't call room service, didn't speak to the maid. Not a word in a week, the maid told the manager (who told my mother), though Aunt Celie stared at her all through the cleaning—it gave her the willies—and she never changed her dress, and there was no hairbrush, no toothbrush, no hair or toothpaste in the sink, though she did go through a lot of toilet paper.

She went there to diet. That's what my mother says, sounding pleased and relieved. That's what the aunts say.

"She went there to hide," I say. From Daniel who was moved last week to Berryhill Convalescent Care Center. It's a place I'm familiar with, where my father died.

"She lost quite a bit of weight," my mother says. The figure passed by telephone: sixteen pounds.

. . .

Small Talk

I WANT TO VISIT DANIEL but I keep putting it off. I have hardly any money. My current attempt at love is in the fragile middle stage now and needs tending. It's been so long since I spoke to Daniel that coming now I would feel awkward, if not vulture-like. I don't want to make it worse for Arthur and Celie.

INSTEAD I IMAGINE HIM in his bed in the nursing home. A friend is coming up the elevator, sneaking up without a Visitor's Pass since only family gets passes into isolation. It's a friend from New York maybe, a gay friend, who also tests serum-positive, who comes with brave, dark jokes about death. Or a lover, tremulous with guilt and fear, with a prescription for AZT or maybe a month's supply of the pills, the one drug that offers hope now, so expensive he took up a collection for it. "It works," the lover says, holding up the little bag to Uncle Arthur in front of the swinging doors to the corridor to Daniel's quarantined room. "It was a miracle," he goes on. "You should have seen Rafe, up and walking around!"

And Uncle Arthur: "Young man, we appreciate your concern."

And when the lover persists, Arthur with tears in his eyes: "Get out of here, will you? Can't you see we're under a lot of strain?" Arms folded in front of the doors which read AUTHORIZED PER-SONNEL ONLY, barring the way to the room, the bed where Daniel lies perhaps lucidly playing and playing again the moment when time stopped fanning out and channeled into the narrow stream which has brought him here. "You can write him a letter," Arthur says. "He'd appreciate that." To this very young-looking man with watery golden freckles over cheeks he doesn't have to shave more than three times a week. To this handsome, nervous Peter Pan of a man of whom Arthur thinks absentmindedly, he isn't Jewish. To his son's lover shredding the moist slip of paper, the white pharmacy bag. To the lover's diffident retreating back.

There is a lover, or was. Two years ago when I was visiting New York with a man who wasn't sure if he wanted to marry me, we met, the four of us, for Sunday brunch at an uptown restaurant with fluffy omelets and a glass of crayons for the paper tablecloths. Steve, my boyfriend, sat with his hands in his lap, a sign of our disconnectedness. Daniel's friend C.J., who looked as if he were still in high school, listened to us respectfully and occasionally stroked Daniel's arm. But Daniel was unhappy. He was oppressed by his new job with *The Fantasticks*. "Musical Director" was a joke when all he did was play the piano, sentimental songs for Midwestern girls who hum along with gum in their cheeks.

"Go West, young man," Steve said. My irritating boyfriend, whom I should have left sooner than I did—my mother thought so—though at the Nanny Rose, I remember, I laughed at his jokes.

"He's going to stick it out," C.J. said. "He's only been here a year. The rest of us type or wait on tables!"

But back in Daniel's apartment after C.J. had gone to the restaurant where he worked, Daniel told us that C.J., his first love in New York, was moving out. C.J. felt Daniel had become too possessive. Daniel was standing at the kitchen counter, his hands pressed flat. "I want to give to him. I want to be for him. What does that have to do with possessing?"

"It's not you," I said. "He's a kid. He's just not ready." Forgiving Steve as well as C.J. Forgiving myself.

Small Talk

Daniel did not take in my attempt at helpfulness. Daniel made sad fun of his love for C.J. (who was actually a year older than he was), comparing it to his father's love for his mother, which his mother had never seemed to return or even acknowledge. Daniel talked right into our eyes as if to force us to see him. He served us tea in gray-blue teacups made of a single sheet of porcelain folded down over itself, and there were Band-Aids on the tips of two of his fingers, and his hand shook on the cup as he described some small nasty act or remark that only someone in his situation would have perceived as nasty, that required a long explanation to be appreciated. Talking past our appreciation in his small pretty apartment, the walls higher than wide or deep, and decorated—in addition to the good prints—with an old eleven by fourteen of his family. It was a hazy color blowup, full sun and a little out of focus, mom and pop kneeling on either side of their maybe ten-year-old boy on sand, a Florida beach maybe. The top of a huge yellow thermos pokes up from the bottom margin, and behind it the vacationers squeeze in for the photo, each holding one of their child's arms—Arthur's chest under his T-shirt already beginning to fall, Celie big-bosomed inside a sweater, and Daniel with a skinny bare chest and a grin wide enough to eat the world, though his parents are clutching his arms so tightly it had to have hurt.

I GET DANIEL'S NUMBER from my mother and I call him. Aunt Celie answers. "He is sleeping," she whispers, the words flattened and curved as if she's smiling into the phone.

I write him a letter with almost no content, since even my biggest problems, reported to him, feel like flexing my muscles of life. I plant my concern between the lines so as not to be depressing. At the end I ask, delicately, if there's anything he'd like me to do for him.

For the next couple weeks I expect something written in the feeble hand of a dying prisoner. I expect words I can barely read on the margin of his weekly menu, stained with tea and Jell-O. *Get me AZT. Get me to a real hospital. Help me.*

I call Uncle Arthur at home and ask how Daniel is. "We're praying for a miracle," he says. "You can never tell, with cancer."

DANIEL IS DEAD. Six hours after getting my mother's message on my answering machine, stopping only for gas, I pull into my old driveway in Cleveland Heights, Ohio. It's early morning and Mom in her robe looks older than I remembered. "Go in and lie down," she says. "I'll unpack for you." She hoists my suitcase over the threshold, then kisses me so fiercely I feel a chill. "What was the hurry? The funeral isn't till tomorrow, didn't I say that?"

"It was murder," I say.

"Mimi, please."

"Manslaughter. Reckless negligence."

I try to explain. It's not that they could have saved him. But once he got sick they wanted him gone. Along with his evil disease. Which proclaimed his sexuality. For which they maybe felt responsible. Because they never made sure he got the right drugs for his condition, which they wouldn't out of their selfish, terror-fed denial even call by its right name! By this time I am shrieking. "He had AIDS! Didn't he?!"

"You know everything," my mother says. "No one can tell you anything."

Yes, no. I know I'm ranting. Mom looks sick to her stomach. But it feels so right and sure (to me who's never felt right or been sure), hating Arthur and Celie and all people who damage the world out of their own weaknesses. And this hate sits hot on my brain and seems to make my eyesight laser-sharp, my inner eyesight onto this scene so vivid it must have happened. While Arthur is at work and Celie is eating a bag lunch in the nursing home lounge and the tape deck on Daniel's nightstand is playing a Mozart piano concerto, here comes C.J. with a bottle of pills and a snapshot of their friend who has AIDS. Daniel lifts his head politely from the pillow. His eyes brush against the eyes of the man in the snapshot, smiling, shirtless, not ill. They move to C.J.'s face, tight with love and guilt and fear for his own life.

"HERE, TAKE ONE!" C.J. says, setting the bottle down on Daniel's tray-table. "Six a day, every four hours. Hardly any side effects, at least not for Rafe."

Daniel mixes up the piano music with C.J.'s words. "Yes," he says to either, to both. And turns his head away, promising to start the medicine when he wakes up. His voice is muffled by the pillow Celie has brought for him, plump with goosedown. "Thanks, babe," he says to C.J. "I love you."

But when he wakes up, the tape will be humming its light, expensive static, and he'll put the pills in the metal drawer in the stand by his bed. He is not interested in this or anything that will prolong what he feels in his parents' blind, frozen smiles. He wanted to give and this is what he has given them: terror. He is swooning in their terror, in the soft, white, gagging down. We're all swooning, drowning, all the cousins from coast to coast, choking on the goosedown of our terrified, imaginary lives.

I'm wrapped in my righteous fury until the funeral service, which his parents observe from a curtained enclosure I can't see into. I hear them though, one of them, a thin wailing, higher, it seems, than the normal range of the human voice, the cry maybe of a small dog. It continues through the eulogy as the rabbi speaks of this young man cut down in the flower of his burgeoning self, the flower just unfurling but already fragrant and so beautiful that God in His sacred mystery... when Celie emerges from the enclosure. The sound fills the room, higher now like the cry of a bat. The rabbi has stopped speaking although his mouth keeps moving, perhaps saying to God what he'd planned to say to the bereaved. Bubby half-rises from her wheelchair in the center aisle and croons, "Shuh, *tochter.*" The sound stops. Celie glances out at the room of mourners with a trace of apology on her face, the slight curl of the corners your mouth assumes outside the door of a party whose hosts are wealthier than you are. Then she lowers herself to the floor in front of the coffin, and my mother beside me grabs hold of my hand, and Celie is on her back on the floor with her knees up and spread apart the way you lie on the gynecologist's table. There is one dead second, one breath, one small gap in the flow of time. Then the sound resumes, in short, evenly spaced beats now, wailing, then ceasing, wailing, ceasing, in time with which Celie raises her hips and then lowers them, up and down, up and down as if she's doing floor exercises or birthing a baby in a dream. I look at the ceiling, at my lap, across the aisle at my aunts looking down at their laps, purses, prayer books, until Arthur helps her up and leads her out of the room.

LATER MY MOTHER will inform me that Uncle Arthur was the soldier who liberated Aunt Celie. And that she could never forgive him for it. That she could never leave him on account of it.

But that's another story, in which I am welcomed into rooms hushed with talk of important things. In this story at the funeral we move lumpily up the aisle, silently. No one seems to be crying. Someone I don't know stops to sign the guest register, a woman, older than I; handsome-looking. I sign my own name, first and last. The air looks gray, feels gritty as if with iron filings, something that should not be breathed, as we push toward the blinding crack of the door.

 Editing

"I just can't go through it again."
—overheard on a bus

Allan wants to marry me. He bought an engagement gift, not a ring, which is too traditional for a second marriage, but a watch, a Seiko, with a Florentine gold band and slashes instead of numbers for the hours. He thinks it will teach me to be prompt. He hopes it will root me more in time, in the real world. That's a lot to ask of a watch.

—It's beautiful, Allan.

—Do you like it? It was on sale, I'd never have been able to get one like this!

Neither of us has money but he flaunts it; he gets visceral pleasure out of special deals.

—Go ahead. Put it on. Put it on!

He's excited. He's never been married before and still believes in the goo, the knee on the kerchief on the floor and the Darling will you please.

—It looks great. You look great. What's the matter, Mimi?

Nothing's the matter. Among other things, I've transcended waitressing. Mornings I make it to Inspiration Films, Inc., find my way to my Movielab. I'm working on a documentary about

Cathedral Pines Youth Camp, a place of reflection for troubled boys ages twelve to sixteen. Teen hoods catch a glimpse of peace beyond understanding. Working title: "Suffer the Little Children."

–So you're functional.

–I like being functional. I crave function.

–So function as my wife.

Poor Allan. He still believes in the fundamental order of things. A code that, if cracked, will afford him control of his life. I'm not so sure. It's ten years since I came back from India. But I still have trouble with certain connectives: "Because." "Thus." Sometimes, even, "And then." I use them tongue in cheek.

–What happened in India, Mim? You never talk about India.

I remember nothing about India because my husband was there. It's a joke, but true, or almost. I retain two mental images. One is the flight out of New York–the bottle of Moët on Michael's tray-table from a stewardess who thought we were nice kids. We wipe our foreheads with the hot washcloths she supplied and hold onto each other's hands. In the second shot Michael is reclining, not against his lowered seatback but a mildewed wall. From time to time, desultorily, his bare foot brushes someone else's, then moves away. The details: his barbarically long toenails; her unnaturally high arch.

Of course, my memory was unreliable even before I got married. Erratically selective, unserviceable for long periods, it would then heave up a flurry of detail, numbers especially. Balboa discovered the Pacific Ocean in 1513. In 1619 slaves and women landed in Roanoke, Virginia. Before Myra Garfinkel moved off my street to go to cosmetology school her phone number was 381-6891, you can call it and check: Cleveland Heights, Ohio.

Editing

−You should see a counselor.

−Do you think so?

−I don't mean a psychoanalyst, just someone to talk to about your marriage phobia.

−You forget two other possibilities: one, that it's the wrong time for me to marry, and two, that you're the wrong person.

−Mimi.

He's trying to bulldoze me. Sweet, meek Allan who learned from his own shrink how to forge his destiny. Michael forged ours. He chose the field where we made love for the first time, on hashish under the night sky; the hilltop farm we bought above a town comprising a post office, a Red Owl and an abandoned gas station.

−You're running, Mimi.

−I suppose you want me to see your own personal Wonder-woman.

−Or we could just talk about it together.

−That would ruin us.

−So let's get to work!

Can I marry him? He has a sense of humor but he's conservative, rational, like my father, who, if he'd lived, would have forbidden me to go to India. Would have put his foot down, though I'd graduated college and married.

Michael was a poet. I found this written on the front cover of one of his notebooks:

Water water in the glass
Molten solid, frozen gas
O that I could ever be
In endless middle state like thee.

Even in retrospect I feel the attraction. He was handsome in a square-jawed, billboard sort of way. He moved slowly and talked slowly and wore a tranquil expression my father would have called arrogance. He was also smart. For three years he passed a full load of Honors Philosophy courses reading the underlined passages in the textbooks of friends. When he finally dropped out, having completed everything but his gym requirement, he was offered a scholarship and turned it down. He was done with Academe and excuses. He wanted to raise bees.

He knew what he wanted, and I had no idea, so we did what he wanted. Once I tried to help him with his poetry. I told him *frozen* didn't bear the same relation to *gas* as *molten* did to *solid.* A more precise word, I suggested, was *liquefied,* as "Molten solid, liquefied gas," no? But he took his notebook away and wouldn't show me any more poems. I can't explain it better than that: he refused to suppress an urge, grand or stupid. He intrigued me, he could unlock worlds for me. He extended my sense of myself; Allan merely reinforces it.

But I can't leave Allan. The thought calls up an ugly flash-forward: bleak truck stop like the one in a movie that depressed me. The title is gone but the scene is lodged in my mind. Boyfriend, a hard, handsome man who makes fun of me lackadaisically, the way people shoot squirrels. He fills our gas tank and I go to the washroom. Sweet-nasty smell. Bugs in the blue water of the toilet bowl. My face in the mirror is chubby, hair tangerine-bleached, and I wonder how I ever came to look like this while he thumbs a ride away from the truck stop and out of my life. Which goes on, with fewer and fewer options. I get a job in a diner, my sense of composition reduced to arranging a plate. I fall for a series of guys of decreasing credibility until an unemployed mechanic named Bud junks me like an old Rambler. Then on the back of one of my checks, my fingers carbon paper blue, I write Allan a terrified plea. It contains grammatical errors and ends, "Don't hate me, I'm fat as a pig." He doesn't answer.

How can he not answer? He's a psychotherapist, or will be. He'd die for me possibly, embarrass himself surely, stay with me no matter what either of us did or wanted. Michael was at best tentative about his commitment. "Love is one of those things you can't legislate," he said. I was sitting on his lap. We used to neck for hours, like adolescents, in a kind of lemon-meringue bliss. "If it comes naturally, like now, it's a miracle. When you demand it, you kill it." In our marriage vows we invoked Fritz Perls and promised to stay together for richer and for poorer, in sickness and in health, as long as the feeling lasted.

–Very entertaining.

Allan's being sarcastic. He doesn't think I've probed deeply enough.

–I'm being as thorough as I can.

He rises from his chair, ponderously, though he's slim and loose-jointed:

–It's glib. That quip about your father, 'would have put his foot down,' don't you have *feelings* for the man?

He turns away as if disappointed in me, then wheels around.

–Now! What's going on with you this moment: January, Tuesday, seven o'clock, come on, you're running out of time!!

We're in the small front room of his apartment. Not much furniture, two chairs, a table, a bowl of fruit. Reduces distraction, as they say, but the simplicity grates.

—It's hard to sound honest, Allan, when someone starts out doubting you.

He shakes my words out of his head.

—You remind me of something.

He scans the room as for some odious object of comparison.

—Imagine a painting in front of a wall safe. You move the picture, try various combinations. But the only way to get into that safe is to blast it open. And what'd happen, do you think, if we did blast it open? What would we find? Stock certificates? Jewelry?

His eyes are almost closed now and he whispers so softly I can hardly hear him:

—What's inside the vault? Is it empty?

—Cut it out, Allan.

He peers down at me. His face is an inch from mine. I can see up his nostrils, the little black hairs, the darkness beyond....

—Tell me about India.

I'm sick of India, the smell of urine in the air and the people squatting alongside the road with nothing to do but ogle the foreign hippies. Too many people, with legs like sticks and smiles that tell you you've sinned, that in some way, social or metaphysical, you're sinning now—against the ricksha driver you overpaid or underpaid, the restaurant you ate the wrong food at, the holy man you failed to recognize.... And the rain which doesn't go away but just stops moving, the drops hanging as vapor under the banana trees, over the yellow mud road....

—The rain, the holy men.

He makes a fist, then opens it, finger by slender finger.

—Go on.

THE NIGHTS IN INDIA. Hot as the days. The populace, it seemed, swarming the roads, steadily, randomly, like blood cells. Transporting mangos? Slave-children? Nothing, usually, which made their movement the more ominous.

Michael was oppressed. He spent a lot of time stoned on a cot in our Bombay hotel room doing the *London Times* crossword. "I don't like to see you down like this," I told him. "Be happy just to be with me. I am, with you."

He groaned. "What am I supposed to say to that?"

"I'm sure you'll think of something. You're creative."

Rolling over, he let the paper fall to the floor. He was thinking much worse than he was saying.

"You know, Michael, there are times when I hate you."

"Sometimes I hate you too," he said, voice muffled against the wall.

"I hate you now."

—GOT TO TELL YOU, Allan, I'm not crazy about this.

Allan's a shithead. My girlfriends, if I told them about it, would bear this out. He's fucking you, they'd say, with the sadist guru bit. Watch out, it's your weak spot.

He kisses my cheek.

—It's hard, especially at the beginning.

Angel slash asshole. It *is* my weak spot. As the past returns in neat, contained memory clots, the present fades out. Not just with Allan. I'm a mess at work. The Cathedral Pines footage doesn't make sense anymore.

—I'm going backward. I'm scared.

—I was too.

—This is me, not you, Allan!

I try to explain. The strips of pictures I handle portray individual actions—a face smiling, legs fording a creek—which it's my job to place in a sequence that makes narrative sense and is nice to look at as well. But yesterday I fed a strip into the machine, planning to glue a shot of one of my War Lords merrily throwing a baseball across a mowed clearing, to a shot of the ball caught—or was it dropped?—and my eyes or my mind shut down. The pictures clicked past me in their little black frames, one square, another square, refusing to meld into one another. They remained separate images—still lifes—a hand at rest, a hand raised, so beautiful and meaningless my own hand froze on the control. No whole, just these arresting, glittering parts.

—Don't you think that's weird, Allan?

—It's a natural phase. It won't last.

—If it doesn't stop soon, Beckman will notice.

—Forget Beckman.

—That scares me too.

THE NEW TEXAS HOTEL was halfway down one of the side streets leading to a larger street that dead-ended in one of the markets. I couldn't find it now. Each time I left it, it seemed a miracle to come upon it again in this life: I had no map and the city was a maze of alleys and plazas; no center I ever did find. The New Texas passed for my center, and I sat up on the roof watching the city and the travelers passing through. We lent some rupees to a young American whose father played the cello in a symphony orchestra, and later learned it was a small neighborhood orchestra, and later still that it was the one my father used to play in; the kid lived six blocks from where I grew up. A robust woman who spoke little English and had no money stayed with us a week and wanted to suck my breasts. Michael said he didn't mind but I wouldn't let her. A Danish woman named Tassia or Jura wanted to sleep with Michael. I said it was OK with me but I combed out my hair, washed all our clothes, and fasted, hoping they wouldn't. I don't think they did. Meanwhile I was losing weight. It wasn't difficult: a single act of will, repeated and repeated. It was harder to carry my pack but that was fine; I went out less. In, out, it was the same, and the perception that it was the same meant I was coming closer to what we'd come for. What had we come for? Something big, no doubt. Probably it mattered even less than in our freest moments when it seemed to matter, and if it did matter, it'd come to us. If you wait long enough, everything will come to you. When we'd been there so long we'd half forgotten we were waiting for anything, a man named Abraham moved into the room next door.

THERE'S A RUSHING NOISE in my ears so loud I can hardly hear my voice. My right shoulder keeps twitching.

—Stand up, Mimi.

I stand. My right arm crooks and pulls backward as if I'm about to throw a ball. The walls of the room are wider at the ceiling than the floor and seem to be moving slowly outward like the petals of a giant mechanical flower. I want to be home on my couch with half a Valium making my studio apartment the warmest, snuggest place in the world. Allan holds out the office fruit bowl. There are three pears. He wants me to select one and toss it to him. My hand hovers over the bowl. Closes over the smallest, green and hard. It's heavy, or else my arm is weak. I can't pick it up.

—It's just a pear.

He picks up all three pears and juggles them for a minute. I didn't know he could juggle. He places a mask over my eyes. Under the mask I see the place in the air where the pears had been.

ABE WAS SHORT for an American man—built like a sturdy preadolescent—but you forgot it as soon as he opened his mouth. At an absurdly young age he'd been elected mayor of some town in southern California. His future looked good—pretty wife, precocious son—when a rumor sprang up connecting him with a Berkeley religious group that practiced something questionable. He was never formally accused; in fact the Sunnymead newspaper printed an article defending him and attacking certain shady interests whose sway over the Sunnymead real estate cartel he was about to challenge, but the thing left a bad taste and one day he threw it all up. He said he was going to the office and went instead to the airport where he bought a ticket for the first flight to anywhere out of the country, landing in Bangkok still so livid with rage, he said, people gave him two feet on either side. He looked anything but livid now sitting cross-legged on my bed, his small hands dancing out his story like birds. He took out a traveling chess set and a timer, and in five minutes beat Michael, who is a pretty good chess player, then turned the board around, took Michael's indefensible position and beat him again, all the while talking about his nervous breakdown in Bangkok, where stumbling through the streets stoned out of his mind (and actually out of his mind), he'd been robbed by the whores; and about the savior who'd taken him to Ganeshpuri and Baba Shivananda–all this related in a voice so ecstatic it had to be phony, because if it was real it was coming from a place I couldn't imagine.

No sound comes to me from behind the mask. I have the feeling Allan has tiptoed out. The door shuts noiselessly behind him. In the morning, still talking, I'm found by the man who comes to clean the apartment.

Once a week in the afternoon Baba's chief disciple would call us into the audience room. It was a quiet, melancholy hour, with a sweetness–us in our freshest saris and dhotis cross-legged on the floor, while light from a high window fell on Baba in his orange robe. He might lecture, translated by one of his Indian disciples. Or we'd sit an hour in silence in the gray light; in Ganeshpuri it rained every day at four.

One day, shortly after Abe arrived, Baba addressed us in English. "Everything in the world, the things we love–" he opened his arms, "–the things we hate–" he wrinkled his nose, "–prasad–" the first gesture repeated, "–and caca–" the second, "–are, how do you say? little movies that fly across our minds with no more permanence than the flight of birds. They are—" Leaning toward Abe, who'd stationed himself near Baba's raised platform, he whispered something, nodded at Abe's reply, then shouted gleefully, "Little soap dramas!" shaking his smooth, butternut-colored body, turning his palm up in the mudra representing devotion to the guru.

The disciples sat bolt upright, the better for the Shakti to rise up the flower stem of their spines. Chandra, the most honored American disciple—from Peru, Maine, she'd said—trembled with the beginnings of Baba-induced involuntary body movements called *kriyas*. She might sit and quiver, or spin down the long room and out the door. Michael waved his hand from side-to-side like the smart-ass in back of the classroom who hasn't read the material but likes to hear his voice. "I've been thinking," Michael said, "in the eyes of God the healer and the murderer are equal. No one beats the other into heaven. Right, Baba?"

The thought was Abe's originally, a revelation that had come to him in Bangkok, he'd told us, but Michael took credit for it, grinning, proud of his question that stumped the experts. Until Baba leaned forward and began retching, several dry heaves, then one which produced a small red-orange stone. The room was as silent as an empty hall. Outside, rain, the monsoon, fell thickly. He emitted another small stone, and then one the size and color of a grapefruit, much too large to have come up through his throat. He didn't seem surprised though; like a child entranced by objects, he gazed at them, knocked them together, held them to his cheek. Then he gave them away, the smaller ones to Chandra and a thin young man who had amoebic dysentery, the grapefruit to Abe. Baba scratched his foot, cocked his head as if listening. He took back Abe's gift, tossed it up several times, then heaved it out over the company, and it fell hard into my hands like a medicine ball.

No one looked at me but I felt pinned by the weight of their attention. In the folds of my sari was a rock, a *vajra*, meaning thunderbolt or diamond, but it was lump rather than crystal, molten and quick-set like lava, and cool to the touch in the hot afternoon room. It made everything around it a little unearthly. I placed it at the foot of my cot between the wooden frame and the mat; that night I dreamed I'd lost faith in the power of gravity.

I want to go home, where horrors are comprehensible. Here flowers bloom and people starve to death as part of some eerie network nobody understands, but all revere. *In distress repeat the name of Rama assiduously.*

—MIMI, WAKE UP.

—Michael?

—You've been talking in your sleep. I should say, you've been bellowing in your sleep.

—Allan, it's you, Allan.

He smells as I remember him. I put my arms around him and try to sleep.

I WAS LONELY AT THE ASHRAM. In our dormitory building Michael and I had to sleep in separate wings. We weren't allowed to converse either. No chitchat. Intercourse between men and women had to be wordless, supra-personal. So I couldn't tell if it was the ashram taboo or his inclination that made Michael spend most of his time with Abe. They sat side by side on the long mat in the dining hall; they swept wide bright leaves from the same path; they meditated on adjacent cushions. One day I found them in the garden together near Michael's favorite statue: Shiva and Shakti fused at the torso, her legs around his waist. Abe was squatting on the flagstones like an Indian. His face upon Michael's was radiant.

"We Westerners," Abe said, "refuse to see that everything ends and comes again."

I knew the rap: our earthly goals are B.S., pleasure is pain, beauty ugliness, all the oppositions that motivate action collapsing to intellectual debris.

"Shiva's telling us," Abe said. "That's why he's holding a skull while he's making love."

"Doctrinaire." Michael was fixed on the statue. "You know they're balling because it feels good."

Abe looked as delighted as if Michael had agreed with him. "They're remarkable, aren't they, Michael? They jolt you out of your ordinary mind, dare you to make the leap into a higher realm of consciousness and join the gods!"

"What the hell kind of leap?" I asked. I hated the idea of Michael joining the gods when he was supposed to be here with me.

They turned to me, allies once more. Abe looked amused. Michael gave me a serene, compassionate look he'd borrowed from Abe.

. . .

—GOOD WORK, MIMI. You're close to something.

—A nervous breakdown.

He kisses the side of my mouth.

—I think we should quit this, Allan. Seriously. You shouldn't know so much about me.

He laughs.

—So far it's not all that X-rated.

He kisses my cheek right next to my ear, a loud kiss.

This therapy is doing great things for Allan. He's more sure of himself; he tells me when he thinks I'm wrong or I piss him off. He looks taller. Jawline more distinct. He blinks less. But the sum of the neuroses of the committed couple is a constant, it seems: I'm not sleeping well and I worry about dumb things. Is my hair clean? Do I smell good? Do I dare impose the artifice of order on the War Lords of Cathedral Pines?

—Allan, let's get married. I'll make an appointment for blood tests. And I want to set things up with another shrink. Your supervisor, maybe. What do you think?

—I think you're running.

MY HUSBAND KEPT ON trying to be a guru. Indian as the Indians, holy as Baba. He told me stories of how the people of Ganeshpuri and even some of Baba's own disciples looked at him with awe, Michael shaking his head as if he couldn't believe it himself. I saw no awe, though he did exert a kind of fascination. I observed it in the eyes of a very young, impressionable French girl, Nathalie, who found it *tout à fait épatant* my husband could be so rebellious. She'd seen him up on the dormitory roof smoking hash which was forbidden here. *Il est fou!* she crooned to me, the pucker accentuating the fullness of her lips, and since she maintained good health in a group ravaged by dysentery, she was one of the few Western women who looked attractive in a sari. Michael was grooming her to be his disciple, and she did small tasks: brought him orders of *samosas* from town, oiled his sandals. One morning, radiant with the pleasure of servitude, she came to me in the meditation hall and summoned me to his presence.

He was sitting at Shiva's feet with the expression people get after powerful movies. "Something's happening to me," he said. "I'm changing." He looked at me tenderly and took my hand but it seemed impersonal and I withdrew mine as soon as I could. "Tell it to Abe." I felt more like a congregation than a wife. In his gauzy shirt and the clean white dhoti Nathalie must have laundered for him, he looked like a fine young Brahmin who'd renounced his caste to ride the third-class trains. He told me that here beside Shiva, from his newly achieved force of will and purity of thought, he'd conjured up a cloud of butterflies with yellow eyes and white-iridescent wings. One of them had landed on his outstretched finger like a tame bird. "The power is here," he told me, hand over his heart. "It's a mistake to look for it anywhere else."

"I feel my morning sickness coming on."

"Just let go." His lips were half-open and he smiled tremulously.

It was frightening. Enlightenment was a race he was beating me at. He'd made a leap and now I'd have to jump after him into nowhere.

. . .

Editing

ALLAN IS ANGRY WITH ME. He says I see him as weak; that I'm still fighting my father so every man who doesn't abuse me seems weak to me; that I'm incapable of a relationship between equals. He paces. Knots in his cheeks form and dissolve.

–I never said you were weak, Allan.

–Spare me.

This is absurd. I used to think of him as too fragile for the world–for myself, actually–but I haven't felt that way in a while. I'm starting to respect him. I tell him so.

–Well, shit. If you thought I was such a mealy little runt, why did you stick with me? If you weren't honest with me then, how can I trust you now?

He's yelling.

–I *was* honest. I wasn't *dis*honest. We don't have to spell it all out, do we? Allan, what's wrong with you?

We've been circling his minuscule windowless kitchen. He walks into the living room. I open the refrigerator, look inside, close the refrigerator. For a moment I think he has gone off. I find him in his counseling room. He looks away as I walk in, but when he turns back to me he seems less angry.

–What do you think happened to you and Michael?

–I don't know. We had different visions. We weren't ready to merge.

He shakes his head, the merest, politest, of disagreements.

–You could have, as you say, *merged*, if you'd wanted to. But you didn't want to. Do you know what you wanted?

He's leaning toward me. His head and shoulders have flattened and elongated, as if I'm seeing through a wide angle lens.

—You wanted to reduce him. You couldn't handle his *power*. You wanted to *weaken him*.

He speaks gently, and I am sinking into a lake of feathers. I want to pull him down on top of me, burrow under his shirt, take his pants off. I want to slap his face, bite his arm till it bleeds.

—You fight anyone stronger than you. You couldn't stand Abraham. You wanted to kill Michael.

I grab a pear and throw it as hard as I can. It hits his leg. I loved Michael—too much. More than I want to think about right now. I want to cry but I don't. The pear has ripened. On Allan's tan corduroy pants there is a damp spot.

TOWARD THE END of my stay at the ashram Abe began to seek me out. His interest surprised me—our conversations hadn't revealed any connection I could see. But Abe was high in the ashram hierarchy, and he was Michael's friend, and my life became infused, if not with happiness, then with a peacefulness I hadn't felt in some time.

Our relationship was correctly supra-personal. I wanted to know what he thought about me and Michael but he avoided the subject, spoke of the marriage of minds, the importance of nonattachment. Once, hungry for the personal, I asked him if he ever felt sexually attracted to me. I did, on occasion, to him. He said he didn't although, if I weren't married, perhaps he would be. "You love Michael, don't you!" I said, not at all jealous, liking that we felt the same way, but he turned clear, bright, and vacant, as if my question had knocked on the door of an empty house. From then on I couldn't think clearly about it.

Michael's whereabouts became less and less known to me. Baba was away visiting the shrine of his own guru, and Michael seemed to have given up the ashram routine. I heard he spent a lot of time in the restaurants and sulfur baths of Ganeshpuri. I saw him walking with Nathalie at the end of the garden. I was jealous then, but only mildly. I was working on nonattachment. I spent my days scrubbing mildew from the flagstone path and the whitewashed steps, chanting the *Bhagavad Gita,* or watching in the darkened meditation hall as my thoughts dance from the sweetness of married love to the rage of a tiger tearing a zebra apart: all one. Abraham told me to bring the *vajra* to meditation and direct my thoughts upon it. This intensified my yoga till I worked, ate, and walked about as on the edge of a cliff–a false step would send me hurtling, and a push, the right push, would empower me to walk on thin air. I took baby steps. I stared at things as if they were new.

One evening after meditation I went for a walk in the garden. It was dinnertime but I was too high to eat, and it was raining a little but the rain didn't bother me; it was body temperature, like sweat. Shiva and Shakti were fornicating away, wet and dark gray, but Michael wasn't there, and as I shifted the rock from hand to hand, I realized I was looking for him. I went to the assembly room. I peeked into the men's dorm. The smell of hash lay sharp and sour on the heavy air. I found him on the edge of the dormitory roof in meditation position. Nathalie sat on his lap with her legs around his waist, naked and glazed with rain like the statue of Shakti. They were laughing, and singing *le jour de gloire est arrivé,*

wagging their bare feet in time to the music, his barbarically long toenails, her unnaturally high arch—and, Allan, if you want a feeling, I can't oblige, because all I felt was a blank, a waiting, as when you light the long cord that leads to the TNT and the flame creeps along over the grass, the concrete, until it rounds a bend on its way to the metal box under the bridge. I wanted to go back to Shiva, to the meditation hall, to America but I couldn't move. I was stuck to the step that opens out onto the roof, absorbed in its whitewash, the blue-green filigree of mildew that grows back two weeks after the scrubbing, and the strains of the Marseillaise,

Aux armes, citoyens! Formez vos battalions!

and I was an Indian, squatting on the top step, feeling no pain though the children have rickets and rain drips in through rusted holes in the shanty roof. I watched the cord burning away, slowly, while the camera cuts to the bridge, the face of the hero, the gathered enemy troops and back again, so I didn't hear footsteps behind me or know who threw the rock that knocked the compound deity off the edge of the roof like a carnival duck. Abe put his arm around my waist, led me downstairs, to a bus for the Bombay airport. It might have been Abe who threw the rock. The spirit of Baba. My right arm strengthened by rage. It could have been anyone. It depends on the editing.

ALLAN HAS BROKEN our engagement. Not because I have it in me to be a murderess but because I won't take responsibility for my past. This is, he says, both function and cause of my erratic memory. I disown my past and consequently my present which will become past. I'd make a lousy wife.

—Are you sure, Allan.

—I don't know. I'm tired.

For a moment I think to fight for him. 1) I'm sorry. 2) I love you. 3) You've got your own marriage phobia you motherfucker. But he looks tired too. We haven't been good for each other.

—Take your watch, Allan.

—Keep it.

—I'd feel weird about it.

—I'd feel weird about taking it back.

—Well, if it'll make you feel better...

—Go to hell.

Beckman has broken with me too. He was appalled by the final edit of "Suffer the Little Children." He felt I'd made an anti-religious statement. I still have no idea what he meant. I'd thrown the takes on the floor, attached them in the order they came to hand. A tribute to time and chance. Which ruleth. *Ecclesiastes.*

And now I'm here on my living room couch, a carton of lemon yogurt on my coffee table and a pack of three by five cards. I write a name on each card: Beckman. Allan. Michael. Nathalie. Shakti. Shiva. Chandra. Myra. Baba. Balboa. The War Lords. The beggars of Bombay. I eat the yogurt and make buildings with the cards and watch them fall, watch them fall. Beckman on Baba. Michael onto Allan. Chandra trips over Myra Garfinkel. Allan joins the War Lords. On crutches for his badly broken leg, which will never heal properly, Michael joins the Bombay beggars. Years later, his dead body floats down the Ganges.

Because. Thus. Then? From now on I make my own films.

❦ The Hand Is Not Ironic ❦

You knew a lot about people from the way they drove. In high school she'd had a guy who wanted to be a boyfriend but he pressed down on the gas, let go, pressed down, let go, so that driving with him was like sailing through choppy seas. She put her book on the floor of the car and rubbed her husband's shoulder with the heel of her hand. "I like the way you drive, Michael."

This was her second husband, who parallel parked in the tightest of spots in a single fluid S-curve, who bought his cars new and took care of them as their odometers passed a hundred thousand, a hundred and twenty, unlike Murray, her first husband, who cracked the engine block of their used Chevy Impala because one cold December night he was too lazy to go out and put in the antifreeze. Besides, Michael loved her in a way she could sometimes feel on the surface of her skin, even when she wasn't with him; and although he wanted a baby and she didn't want a baby yet—if ever—so far he'd been patient with her. She liked how the sun slanting in under the visor made the veins stand out on top of his hand. "You're good behind the wheel, Michael," she said louder.

Then, "What do you say when someone says something nice to you? *Michael?*"

"*Sara?*"

He mimicked her intensity. She hated that. Loved it. She said, "I'm not going to have fun this vacation."

"You're not supposed to have fun," he said. "This is *my* family. I don't have fun at your parents' in Boynton Beach."

"You *do* have fun! I know you. You just pretend you're not, to lay up guilt points."

He laughed and poked her under the arm. She poked under his arm. He caught her hand, chewed on the fleshy base of her thumb, then kissed it. She felt his breath, the prickle of his mustache. The car veered slightly. "Be careful," she said, though she had no real fear of an accident with him. In her imagination he could drive and read at the same time; he could drive and make love to her. "At least," she said, "in the Flamingo Palms Retirement Community you don't take your life in your hands."

As he detailed the dangers of golf carts and weekly insecticide sprayings, not to mention bridge with her father, she thought about what she was really afraid of. Not white-water canoeing, which seemed too mythical to frighten her, but the feeling she got from certain kinds of people, burning her throat for weeks afterward with a sour, potatoey ozone. She'd met them last summer at her and Michael's wedding–Ann, her new sister-in-law, silent at the head table, her face cold and brave like a captured spy's: Ann Boleyn. Annie-Get-Your-Gun. And Ann's husband Peter, whose uninflected, nasal voice gave everything he said a double meaning. Peter was short, with a lean face and pinkish hair. He sent back the fish entrée that had been ordered especially for him and asked piously—or was it ironically?—for a second baked potato. Saint Peter. Peter the Great. Peter Pan. They both had degrees from good colleges but afterward had joined a religious cult (religious *group*, Michael said), the thought of which did not intrigue, but bored her. Now they lived in a house they'd built all by themselves on the edge of a dying town and did something reclusive and naturey like watching for forest fires, as if you got extra points for making it in the world with one hand tied behind your back. "Do you think your sister is pretentious?" she asked Michael.

"Less pretentious than you," he said.

"At least I have good clean honest pretentions. They pretend they're for real. That's what's dangerous."

Michael laughed. She reflected pleasurably on her cleverness. But she wasn't fully assuaged. She had recently learned that Ann was pregnant, and the only women she disliked more than new mothers were pregnant women. And even though she knew herself well enough to recognize in her dislike something of fear, her fear annoyed her—even thinking about the fear. She wanted nothing so badly as to be back in Chicago, drinking cappuccino at a sidewalk restaurant, eating an almond croissant and telling her girlfriend Bonnie the psychological minutiae of her trip west. She pictured it: Bonnie's white crushed cotton summer top and, under the table, her own straw purse bulging with her book and her journal in case Bonnie came late.

But Bonnie was three turnpikes away and receding, so Sara picked up *Women in Love* and tried to deduce the primal scene, the unconscious traumatic event that, according to Lacan and the new

Freudians, generated each fictional text. This was for a course in modern British literature she'd taken that spring and hadn't completed. She had an Incomplete. She felt incomplete, missing, besides her final paper, a set of tonsils, several contact lenses, a deaf white cat with one blue eye and one green eye, a first husband. But with the book on her lap—emblem of her career, of a respectable working persona—the possibility of completion loomed like the sign WELCOME TO COLORADO (Please Drive Safely) flashing past them now, and she was hopeful; she could learn things.

OR COULD SHE? Peter gave her a hard hug that ended all at once, leaving her to find her balance. Ann flashed her a glance over a colander of what looked like weeds, then turned away as if depressed by what she saw. Ann was beginning to "show," all her cells swollen with liqueur de female; Peter seemed, if possible, leaner than before, stringy muscles hard as the sole of a boot—bodies sufficient unto themselves. Eastern European faces, unsmiling.

At the kitchen table, perspiring in the afternoon heat of Grand Junction, Colorado, she waited for one of them to introduce a topic of general interest. They discussed their vegetable garden, an upcoming meeting against nuclear something or other, the kitchen floor Peter had recently laid, in unglazed earth-colored tiles, the amnio Ann had refused to have although it was recommended for her age group. Ann was older than Michael and supposedly smarter, although it was hard to see, watching her. Sara drank rosehip iced tea, scratched a bug bite she didn't remember getting, sat very still so as to keep the sweat in her body from seeping out of her pores.

Michael tried—she appreciated it—to make a place for her in the society of his family. He touted her GRE scores, allowing her gracefully to confess the course she hadn't finished, the paper she couldn't write that was due at the end of the summer. She wouldn't have minded describing to them how hard it was to teach and study at the same time or how much she liked—and was still a little awed by—the Ph.D. program she'd finished her first year of, but they didn't even feign interest, and she felt oddly disembodied, simultaneously superior to them and inferior, a stance her friend Bonnie's shrink said made for trouble.

Dinner was eggplant lasagna, which wasn't bad, and lettuce from the garden, which tasted bitter and left sand in her mouth. Afterward Peter passed around a sour, heavy beer called Old Peculiar "for the rehabilitation of the overeducated," he told her, grinning as if to say he had her number. Now the mood changed. "Sara"—he kept saying her name—"Sara, have you ever gotten really ripped?" And, "Sara, is there anything you'd give your life for?"—questions that weren't really questions.

"I got drunk once on sake when I was into Zen and threw up in our bathroom sink," she said. "Is that a sign of my free spirit?" Peter laughed, which pleased her. But really, she told herself, why give any credence at all to the opinion of someone you don't care for?

The sound of her voice in the room at last, or maybe the beer began to soothe her. Peter said some funny things. She noticed that, from certain angles, in a Heidi-goatgirl sort of way, Ann looked almost beautiful. When the conversation turned to the river trip she relaxed still more. She took notes and drew up a list for the equipment they had and another for what they needed. There was a rubber raft for her and Michael, reportedly safer than a canoe. She pictured them bobbing between boulders over water white as the head of a million beers, and chanted to herself the river-safety rules Peter had just laid out for them: (1) Stay with the boat, and (2) If you can't stay with the boat, go down the rapid on your back, feet first. Ah, physical fear, so much cleaner than mental.

Perched on a step stool at the kitchen table with her second beer, she was almost enjoying herself when another couple showed up with their guitar and their chubby blond two-year-old. Michael began making faces at the little girl, who was called Baby Emmy. Baby Emmy walked over to one of the cupboards and took out a saucepan, lids, a grater. She brought the grater over to Michael. "Thank you," Michael said, "I've been wanting a grater."

"She likes you," Emmy's mother said to Michael.

Baby Emmy was in love with Michael. Sara did not care for Baby Emmy, her cabbage cheeks, her wide open eyes that didn't stop moving. The newcomers sat down on the uneven red-orange floor, leaned back against the homemade, linseed-oiled cupboard doors, and discussed the words Emmy was learning to say (there weren't many), and U.S. international politics, in which they found the usual consummate wickedness, and the local environment, for which the locals had no concern or appreciation. Last week on the edge of his ten acres Peter had found an auto garbage bag spilling cans, juice boxes, cigarette butts, and a torn envelope. He'd trucked the bag, cigarette butts and all, over to the address on the envelope and handed it to the woman who answered the door. "You left your belongings on my land," he'd said, banging his knee now with the glee that her first husband Murray had displayed over Watergate.

Michael laughed so hard he started to squeak. Sara would have laughed too but she felt sorry for the woman standing at the door with the garbage in her hand.

Smiling stiffly, arms folded across her chest as she'd learned not to do in a job interview, Sara sat on her step stool slightly above and outside the conversation. Michael was talking to Peter's friend about a news item from "All Things Considered." Both men had heard the news item, remembered all the details; neither had anything to add to the other's store of information. They found this terrifically funny. Sara was schooling herself to be less scrupulous about what came out of her own mouth when Baby Emmy walked over to her. "So what's going on, Emmy?" she said gruff-heartily, as she'd heard adults talk to children. "Are you enjoying the party?"

Baby Emmy stood staring up at her with her mouth slightly open. Sara's hand went to her hair, then she noticed the child's gaze was aimed lower. "That's my *necklace,*" she said, enunciating to enlarge the child's vocabulary. She leaned forward to give her a better look.

"Mine!" said Baby Emmy.

Sara shook her head gently. "It's mine, honey. It's fragile. Here, take *this.*"

She offered Emmy a key ring from her purse. The child gave it a single cold glance, then returned her gaze to the necklace, a string of small silver beads that Sara liked to wear with dark-colored T-shirts. The child's mother was talking to Ann, and Sara couldn't remember her name. "Mine!" said Baby Emmy, her chubby arm reaching, her voice rising to a wail. Bad seed, Sara thought. Monster child.

"Hey, Sara," Peter called out. "What have you done to the lit-tle girl?"

"Oh, shut up, Peter."

She tried to make her voice as flat as his but side conversations had stopped. All eyes were on her, the accused, the truly petty bourgeois, valuing possessions over personal relations. Emma made short bleating sounds, jumping up and down on one leg. Sara gave out what felt like a demented smile.

Emmy's mother came over and murmured to the child, who let herself be led away backward, her bleats subsiding. Sara sat on her stool with her head up, a stiff hand on each knee. She would have taken off the necklace; it wasn't that rare or that expensive. But it was linked now with a small but crucial nugget of herself. If she had done what had seemed to be required of her, it would have felt like drowning.

With the necklace inside her shirt and the subject changed, she learned Emmy's mother's name: Denise. But she still felt off bal-ance. Familiarity hummed in the room, shared views that stood out against her like a wall—what was she doing here? It was clear they all knew each other better than she knew anyone except Michael. And maybe better than she knew Michael, because when you came down to it, how well did they know each other? After five untroubled years of marriage, Bonnie's husband had said he didn't love her anymore, and in the midst of these people Sara didn't know or want to know that she heard with clear and unspeakable horror: I don't love you. I'm sorry but I don't love you anymore, I love Denise now—she tried out different names—I love Meryl Streep now. Princess Di now— From time to time Michael gave her

facts to help her follow the conversation: "That's the girl he was living with when he drank the entire bottle of soy oil." "That's the
head of the food co-op who fifteen years ago walked barefoot
across Turkey!" Michael was having a great time. Finger and
thumbpicks making his right hand witchy, he jigged up and
down the neck of Peter's guitar while Peter scraped away at a little mandolin, with his friend on a gaudy twelve-string. Wafting
up from below was cute-kiddie talk, rough-labor-and-delivery
talk, the women murmuring together, and she suppressed the only
contribution she could think of, "Yes, well, I had an abortion
once." Baby Emmy emptied a box of crayons onto one of the floor
tiles and put them back with heartbreaking carefulness. Sara sat up
straight on her stool, doing nothing, thinking nothing, feeling nothing except, from time to time the tickle on the side of her leg from
the end of Peter's mandolin string, and staring from time to time,
since no one was watching her, at the curly hairs on the calf of
Peter's short blond leg, which curled with a perkiness that felt
intentionally abrasive.

"SARA?"

She awoke on the foam rubber mattress in the unfamiliar living
room to find Michael running his hand slowly along her side, over
the curve of hip. He'd taken off his T-shirt; she felt the hair of his
chest against her back, his penis against the top of her thighs, courteous, tentative.

But she was tired. She had been dreaming. She could not get
up and rummage through her suitcase for her diaphragm. She

turned her face to him, murmuring, "I lost my contact lens and I had to fish through all the dust and hair in this vacuum cleaner bag and at first I thought I'd found it but then I saw the bag was full of contact lenses, a green the size of an eyeball, a tiny pale blue, a clear one with a crack. There were hundreds. I had no idea which was mine."

"Terrifying."

He was kissing her face with sweet, chaste junior high kisses, which needed only a movement from her, the slightest relaxation of the muscles of her back, to turn pressing. She kissed him delicately, remotely, with little tugs backward, away. Please, not now. Please, I'm sorry. But he didn't get it. Chose to ignore it. Pressed harder.

"It feels weird in their living room," she said.

"Yes," he said. "Sexier."

"I don't know where my diaphragm is."

"Forget your diaphragm."

"I need it."

He ceased kissing her so abruptly she felt a chill. He turned away, placing her behind him, and she felt behind, left out, and tried to fit her body to the planes and curves of his back. It was dark out, the everlasting middle of the night.

ON THE BOW SEAT of the rubber raft, legs up on one inflated side, head resting on the other, she watched the slow drift of rust-red canyon wall, the narrow road of sky above.

She felt subdued, convalescent. Michael wasn't that talkative either. But she could see he was loving the trip, the arm and chest action of rowing, the 3-D world gone 2-D, flattened to bands of sky and water. She tried to see what he saw, absorb herself in the tall slim fingers of rock called Fisher Towers, and beyond, the shadowy snowcaps that at certain turns broke softly into sight like a bird touching down.

"Michael, are you angry with me?"

"Why should I be angry with you?"

"You shouldn't be angry."

He laughed. "Now that you remind me, it's coming back to me, all the bad things you've done on this trip." He pulled back on an oar. A cat tongue of water licked her shoulder.

"That *I've* done!" But she said it almost to herself, lying back against the pillowy side of the raft, trailing her hand in the brown water. Spermy water, a Lawrence term. And right for this part of the Colorado River, pulsing in easy waves over boulders well below the surface. Nice here. Solitary, with Ann and Peter Pan in the canoe too far ahead for chitchat. Even straining at the oars Michael couldn't catch them. He rowed hard, and the raft veered wildly to one side. He pulled slow and steady; the raft slogged forward as if through mud. "Pig!" He sounded frustrated. The pace was fine with her. She willed the current even slower, conjured up a sandbar, something to keep them to themselves alone in this little connubial boat.

Ahead, the canoe had vanished into the point on the horizon where the banks met. Rounding the bend she saw it again, docked in a sandy stretch between two rocky outcroppings. Peter was rummaging for something under the sprayskirt. Michael veered toward the bank where Ann sat motionless, her feet in the water.

On land it was hotter than in the middle of the river. Ann's skin looked pale under her sunburn. "We could use a stronger sunblock," Sara told her. "I once had some oily stuff made for sailors marooned in the Pacific. That might work here." Ann didn't answer, didn't change expressions. Sara touched her arm. "Are you all right, Ann?"

"I'm great."

Sara couldn't tell whether the response was courageous or sarcastic; she struggled to stay sympathetic while Peter brought the canteen and a bag of trail mix. Ann had got herself dehydrated, Peter said with his drawl that seemed to mock itself. "A little salt should do it. And forget paddling for now. You ride the raft." Sara watched his fingers fumble-open the cellophane bag. His hands were large on his arms, with clipped nails and thickish wrists, hands like the heads of small clubs, but there was such assurance in his caretaking, such an unequivocal assumption of responsibility she felt a little breathless. Michael of course would have been just as concerned and assured. But she wouldn't have let him, she would have fought him.

The sun glinted green on the brown water, and the sharp, skittering points of light brought tears to her eyes. She counted how many more days of this, days before she can come home to argue in vivid and accurate prose that *Women in Love* had no suppressed primal scene. In *Women in Love* the primal stuff was oozing all over the surface, with Gudrun virtually murdering her husband in her quest for full female power. Had other critics seen that? What had she failed to see?

She resurfaced to learn that she had been assigned to Ann's

place on the canoe. A pulse of excitement began to tick in her throat. She took Michael's hand. "With Michael at the helm. He's a superior pilot!"

Peter looked leery, made Michael demonstrate the J-stroke, which Michael apparently performed competently. "I took boating at Red-Raider Day Camp," she said. "Friday from two to two forty-five." Peter didn't laugh; he was looking at the map. He'd never canoed this part of the river, he said, but it looked all right, class one and two rapids, big waves but no rock gardens; piece-a-cake. There was only one spot to watch for, five or six miles down. Friends had told him about it—happened last year in a flash flood. Rapid so new it wasn't marked yet. He showed them where it would be and described the problem, a sheer rock wall, to their left. "Walls you got to watch for," he said. "They get worn away underneath and have this nasty trick of sucking you toward them. Don't worry. Just paddle hard and keep right."

IN THE CANOE SARA FELT more powerful than she was accustomed to feeling. Every shift of her weight, every change in the speed or rhythm of her paddling affected their balance and direction. She stopped paddling and bounced gently on her seat, laughing as the canoe jumped in the water. "Are you okay?" Michael called out.

"I'm fine! Great!"

Under the sprayskirt her body had vanished from the waist down, become a giant buoyant torpedo-shaped tail; tiny waves hit the waterproof material and flowed back into the river. She breathed evenly, feeling her life jacket snug across her back. She was part of something well-designed; very tight. It was particularly nice riding in the front seat—sky and water her own discovery, her silhouette the focus of her husband's landscape. She almost told him, then hugged the words to herself and paddled hard to the count of ten. The canoe veered toward her paddle hand.

"Sara, what are you doing?!"

"Nothing!"

She was breathing hard, the sweet ache in her paddle arm subsiding sweetly. This was much better than the raft. She felt so strong, so self-reliant she was beginning to wonder whether the outcast feeling was imaginary, the produce of riding a bad boat, just as, when she'd gone from junior high into high school and lost weight and worn Bobbie Brooks instead of the original creations from her mother's sewing machine, she'd managed to become almost popular. She was thinking about this, feeling almost sorry for Ann and Peter, who had voluntarily restricted the scope of their achievements. Then she thought about her paper, trying to find an angle which included her analysis of Gudrun's character but which would place the issue in a larger perspective, maybe open it into a doctoral thesis, and when she saw the wall it looked a lot smaller than the wall in her mind. The waves alongside it looked bouncy but gentle. The river was wide here, and to the far right there were almost no waves at all. She was a little disappointed.

They were in the middle of it with absolutely no sense of having entered. Water boiled, sounded like a freight train, but she wasn't scared, telling herself what Peter had said: Paddle hard, beat the current, stay in charge. But hard as she paddled she knew she wasn't in charge, and Michael wasn't in charge, with the water boiling around the boulders; they were in the midst of boiling soup. She paddled ferociously, struck a rock, pushed off, paddled. By a hair they missed a bad rock that wanted to crack them in two like a peapod, but another rushed at them, and as she reached out with her paddle to give it a push, to do something to determine their destiny, there was a nasty little crunch, and a jolt about as bad as when Murray fell asleep in stop-and-go traffic and hit the car in front of them.

The air was frantic with sound and spray, water pouring at them loud as the subway, but they weren't moving. They had stopped. The canoe, turned sideways, made a perfect right angle to the current, pinned to the rock by the current's force. It was almost funny, how still they sat in the midst of mayhem. She turned around to see if Michael had any more ideas than she had, started what might have come out as "This is amazing!" when the canoe began to tilt away from the rock, so slowly that until she hit the water she believed that leaning the other way would have an effect.

It was the oddest sensation in the world. Hands of water pushing at her back, her arms, pulling at her clothes; a gang of wild men trying to rip her from the boat and dash her to pieces on the rocks downstream. They snatched her paddle; she yelped once at the little loss. But the boat was still pinned to the rock and now she had two hands free; she held as tight as she could to the rope that held the sprayskirt, kicking against the rush of water. She tried to wrap her legs around the bow but the fiberglass was slippery, and she flapped back and forth like a skirt on the line, calculating how long she thought she could hold on with her hands alone. The number five came to mind. Minutes? She was scared, she knew, but with only part of her mind, and the other part felt the wind on her face, heard the water roaring, thought sadly of her Incomplete, saw the raft bob safely by, Ann and Peter looming for a minute, then receding into tiny painted dolls.

These thoughts and pictures followed close upon each other, leaving no space for checking the stern of the boat for someone holding on like crazy. She was holding on like crazy, forcing her mind on her hands, on the sun air water, on what she was thinking about just before they breached. It was an interesting subject, worth pursuing. Something about keys, a lock, a keyhole, something shaped like a keyhole, which, enlarged, became a guitar, no, a mandolin with its round body and slim neck. Murray played the mandolin and he had a sweet voice, better than Michael's although she'd never say so. The water was so loud it was hard to hear the song but there was a light overhead, the flat silvery light on the dentist's ceiling and in her hand a button to press that the dentist said would stop the pain of the drilling better than Novocaine, just press when it starts to hurt; and she pressed, and it made a whooshing sound in her ears which got louder the harder she pressed, but the pain shot higher still, incredible pain, like the time Murray and a girl years younger than she was even then, too young for Murray. Murray and this girl played music together, beautifully, guitar and mandolin, their voices strong, clear, terribly sweet. Then afterward in the living room, she, Sara, sitting on her beanbag chair, in her chair newly pregnant, not showing yet but round in the face, a little puffy—and they across the room on the couch holding hands right in front of her, as if they were the married couple with their not-quite baby and she the little hippie groupie folksinger Murray had met after his show and brought home to jam with. She didn't complain to Murray, adhering to the then-ethic that jealousy was no feeling to admit to yourself let alone tell someone, but she was sick to her stomach, and she felt it again in the boiling water. Pictures were gone. Nothing but the boat under her hands, slippery wet and too large to hold onto. Under the water her legs pulsed like cloth. Terrified flimsy fingers. Not a strong swimmer despite Red-Raider. Michael?

AS THE IMAGE OF MICHAEL in trouble broke upon her mind, loosening her handhold, she saw Peter in the water upstream, half swimming toward her, half hurled by the current. He grabbed onto the canoe, heaved himself up and began inching toward her, stretching a leg backward, a knee forward along the canoe's slippery side. His hand felt almost dry and so large around her wrist that she went light as a twig and he pulled her up easily. She crawled after him along the side of the canoe, one hand, one knee, the other hand, other knee, her arms and legs shaking in steady slow-motion pulses. Even on the relatively flat surface of the rock her shaking went on slow and steady, and he patted her arms, rubbed her calves over her wet cotton trousers. Her legs were shaking too much for her to stand but raising her head she saw Ann threading her way toward them up the bank. Behind Ann, downstream where the rocks ceased and the river widened into an eddy Michael stood in water to his waist, waving to her. The sting of joyous relief was gone almost as she named it; across the boiling river he seemed to inhabit another dimension. Ann was clambering along the rocks of the nearest bank, close enough for Sara to see the blue of her T-shirt drying pale in the sun.

Ann's mouth was moving with encouragement or advice, but the current was too fast for them to swim to her, and too loud for them even to hear what she was saying. There were two worlds now—the shore, the world at large, in large, and the rock, this little space maybe two feet by three feet, where she and Peter would live from now on, eating food salvaged from the canoe, not talking or talking with their hands because no one could hear anything over the noise of the river. She crossed her legs for a firmer seat on the rock. But Peter was motioning forward, into the cauldron, downstream between the high sharp rocks to the eddy beyond. It was the way Michael must have been swept. It must be possible for the human body to submit to that ferocity without being damaged. She screamed, though she couldn't hear herself, "No no no no no!"

Peter's mouth made a word. She screamed as loud as she could, "I can't!"

His mouth moved again. She thought he was saying "Trust me," or "Trust it!" which sounded ironic to her even though she couldn't hear it. She looked down but her glance hit the water and flicked off. Nowhere to rest.

He took hold of her arm and pulled her up so that she was standing beside him. His hand on her arm was not ironic. He was even shorter than she had thought, her own height, but firm on the rock like a barnacle, and she wanted to kiss his hand—pathetic slavish harem-girl gesture, she hated the idea, she loved it. Instead she kissed him, put her tongue in his mouth, and she loved his tongue, his teeth, the warm inside of his mouth. Then, with the warmth thrumming on her own lips and tongue, she slid down the front face of the rock into the terrible water.

❦ Fossilized ❦

What would you like me to call you?" Vivian looks at the name on her roster: Kim Jeong Soo. There's a rule, she knows, though she can't remember it now, for which of these three Korean names is the first name.

The student looks pleasantly straight in front of her, as if to say whichever name the teacher prefers she'll be happy to accept. Her face is not what Vivian thinks of as pretty. Vivian gazes at her broad, flat forehead and wide-bridged nose, trying to see through what might be her own vestigial racism. "Kim?" she says. "Soo?"

The student maintains her agreeable expression. Vivian looks for a transition to the next activity, can't find it. Some of the other students, all of whom have been sitting with the first day's somewhat slumbrous attention, begin to stir. A boy named Alexander Dixon, who wants to be called Alexander and not Al or Alex, takes out a novel from the *Atlantic Monthly* series and starts to read. A boy named Neil Applebaum, who also wants to be called Alexander (it was his middle name: Neil Alexander Applebaum, he announced with a fake British accent that might have been earnest but might also have been satirical), leans back in his chair and stretches ostentatiously. Vivian wonders what Paul would do, her husband, who got her this teaching job, on different days than his, so one of them could be home at all times with the babies. During Vietnam Paul taught seventh grade on the West Side of Chicago; is utterly sure of himself in front of his classes. Vivian's class appears to be looking at her with a single faceless obtuse arrogance. Her voice gets higher, sharper, more painfully forceful.

PAUL'S OFFICE IS A TINY ROOM next to the nursery. It's the only room with an air-conditioner, which blots out the noise of babies, telephone, ambulance, and fire trucks (their apartment is near a fire station) along with the summer heat. But it's fall now, a cool September morning, as, coffee in hand, Paul walks down the hall to recommence the play he's been working on and which so far he's pretty excited about. The babies, praise the Lord, are strolling outside with the sitter.

He has a bad feeling even as he puts his hand on the doorknob. The hook and eye that he installed last month are disconnected. And yes, piled on his desk but in a heap, not as he himself left it yesterday morning, are the three Xeroxes of his play (one blank, one with his own corrections, one with comments from a more successful writer-friend). The top page is 56. The page with his name, address, and *Baby Zombies from Hell* (working title) is nowhere to be seen. He doesn't have to look farther to know that Jerome's comments are inextricably mixed with his own (both in pencil), and that it will take him two-thirds of the morning, two-thirds of the limited amount of baby-sitting that he and Vivian, with their part-time teaching jobs have decided they can afford, to restore it to an order he can work with. He can't even begin the sifting now, picking out the three page ones et al.–he is too full of the scenario of this small vandalism–the phone ringing in his room, Vivian answering and then forgetting to relock the door, and then fussing around in the bathroom or with a book, oblivious to Nora and Benjamin up from their naps, jubilantly ransacking. He feels all the angrier since his wife somehow manages to order her time so that she has time–for friends, tennis, her doctoral work, occasional (he imagines) proto-flirtations with male students. "I'll destroy your disks," he and Vivian have threatened each other in the midst of fighting, part joke but partly the only satisfying vengeance, the worst punishment either of them can think of to inflict on the other because their disks contain all their written labor for the three years since they bought their twin computers.

He doesn't destroy her disks, though. At the other end of the hall, on her desk in an alcove of the living room, he picks up the first chapter of *Circles of Time: A Study of Repetition in the Work of William Faulkner and Gabriel García Márquez* and throws it at her bookcase. The act gives him no pleasure. He walks back to his room furious with his new mental picture–of Vivian so busy and happy she'll wonder if she didn't scatter the pages herself maybe reaching for a book.

VIVIAN COMES HOME wanting soup, its fragrance suffusing the air of the apartment, blotting out her teaching day, fusing together the fragile components of her family. She sets down her bag of groceries on the mat in the hall, unlocks the door. "Paul? Angel-pies?"

Her voice resounds with mother-warmth. Paul, she knows, feels that their life has deteriorated since the babies. This is one of their current arguments, whether things have gotten better or worse for them, but for her there is no question. She is still astonished by the ease with which she can forget unpleasant past events as her children come hurtling toward her across the rug. No one, not even Paul, has ever been so unequivocally happy to see her. "Nora? Benjie-pie?"

Grocery bag in her arm she stalks down the hall, stops at the door of the nursery. One of the twins is screaming. Dropping the bag, she rushes in, picks up Benj, whose face is pale mottled red as if from age-old, unassuaged grief. Nora is miraculously asleep.

"Paul!" she cries, pulling open his door. Paul's back is toward her. She thrusts the child at him like Agamemnon's bloody robe. "Paul, didn't you *hear* him!" Her voice is full of reproach but whispered so as not to alarm her son who is looking around the room with a grin on his face. Perhaps the whisper was too soft and weak to convey her outrage. Paul continues pat-patting his computer keys as if alone in the world. She squeezes Benj to her chest.

In the living room she sees the pages of her dissertation scattered on the rug. "How could you, Benjela?" she says, kissing the side of his head. She isn't angry with Benj, whose attempts at exploration, however destructive, she finds utterly charming. She isn't even that angry at Paul now, whose acts of passive aggression, however outrageous, do not assault the vulnerable heart of her.

Each time he does something she would call irresponsible she feels pressure on the little place where she keeps her love for him, but although the place has been pushed farther and farther back from her awareness, it is so far intact. She asked him once, after a fit of anti-family rage in which he'd thrown a piece of their wedding china at the refrigerator, "Aren't you afraid I'll get fed up with you?" He had broken the bowl, dented the almond-painted door panel. Every once in a while just after awakening she fixes on the veins in his eyes, pores in his skin. But so far these spells of remoteness concern her no more than a mild headache after a hard teaching day. They will subside, she is sure, as Nora gets old enough to fall in love with her father, and Benj to play catch with him in the park. She sets her son down on the kitchen floor and starts to chop vegetables, stepping adroitly around the pans he has taken out of the cupboard.

PAUL'S MAIN CHARACTER is a newborn baby to be played by an adult male in a diaper. The baby is fully articulate and conscious of having ruined his parents' lives, exuding a faintly evil glee that Paul had originally imagined as comic. Now, however, unable to strike the right lightness of tone, Paul thinks of Jory Dwyer. In the days of his first, less congruous marriage he would hanker for Jory, the most ethereal, well-read, and physically attractive member of his graduate writing program, although he was never sure how much his attraction was fueled by his first wife's righteous possessiveness. He and Jory drank a lot of morning coffee together before the workshop, and yes, there was the pleasurable pain of the way she'd turn her head around quick on her neck to see who had just come into the room, and her exquisite sentences of a poet. But he did not sleep with Jory ten years ago and he does not want her now, really, her pale gray sloe eyes, her fragile, almost immaterial, pale brown hair, her sentences shimmering with palely luminous suggestion. He wants Vivian, who beats all her friends at tennis and makes precise, directed statements. Vivian, who wasn't married before, who doesn't know what it's like to have once rooted yourself in something that shifted. Vivian is six years younger than he, not a huge gap, he'd thought, although he seems to have aged while she remains as she was when they met; in pictures he thinks (no one says) that she looks like his daughter. He wants to make love with Vivian, feels himself desiring her, but reluctant because, since the children, there has been this reluctance in her. She seems to have turned mentally virgin—motherhood obliterating all her desire for sensual touch except for the soft, sweet skin of her children.

"WHY ALL THIS ORWELL STUFF?" says one of the Alexanders. He wants to know why there are three essays by George Orwell on the syllabus and only one by each of the other authors.

The two Alexanders are seated at opposite ends of the long table, one at her elbow and the other, who questioned her, across from her at the farthermost distance. She's not sure yet which is which—none of the students have differentiated themselves except for the Korean girl she has decided to call Kim and the single black student, Stephen White, who wears a red bandana and a gold earring in the shape of a Jewish star. The boy who challenged her has a cherubic blond face that would look adorable in a responsive student. "Why do we have to single out one guy as the essay king?" he says, jerking one of his eyebrows up in the air, a display of muscle control that makes him look like an evil cartoon character. He says, "Isn't this a democracy?"

Vivian is charmed by the term "essay king," but not his tone of belligerence. But before she has a chance to suggest that even in a multicultural democracy one is allowed his/her preference, a girl with red licorice twists of hair to her waist and a large straight nose like Glenn Close's raises her hand. "We had to read Orwell in high school. Frankly, I'm tired of dead white males."

"What's wrong with being dead?" says the Alexander beside her, entwining his fingers behind his head. His glance grazes the redhead, then comes to rest on blond Alexander down the table, as if he's the real antagonist. The Alexander beside her is dark, hunched, greasy-haired, almost emaciated, the way she pictures Dostoevsky's Raskolnikov. With more than ordinary passion, he speaks of Orwell's lucid prose, and something in his delivery seems to irritate the other students. Blond Alex rebuts, others chime in, Vivian watches Kim's eyes bob from one to another with frantic respect. "Could you yell one at a time, please?" Vivian asks, but no one seems to hear.

There is too much energy in the room, Vivian thinks. Too much frustrated longing. Too little repression. As a T.A. at the state university where she is getting her doctorate she met the threat of dissidence by talking fast, giving lots of work, and preparing inordinately, a procedure which sailed her over the first three or four weeks, and later, if a challenge arose–it rarely happened–she'd garnered enough resources in the form of student errors in logic, syntax, grammar, and fluency to justify (to herself) the fact of her authority.

Here, though, it's as if she has gone into battle without her body armor. "Orwell is a stunning writer." It's all she can say, enclosing the girl and blond Alex in the mesh of her gaze. Alex's face is slack, his voice chilly cold. "Isn't that a matter of opinion?" he says, slouching back in his seat as if he's a million years old.

Keeping her voice and face scrupulously pleasant Vivian explains that not only does Orwell write beautiful sentences, he cares about how the world is run, but even as she speaks she is aware that cherubic Alexander is not concerned about the reading list. He hasn't bought either of the textbooks. This is his toss of the glove, his initial ruffling of the water between him and her. He is her nightmare student, bright and unforgiving, pledged heart and soul to fighting her for control of the classroom.

Later, collecting the papers Vivian sees that dark Alex's is longer than that of the other students', with right as well as left-justified margins, and she dubs him Alex the Good. Kim's paper is written on lined notebook paper in a child's clear, round printing. "I am *no good* writer," the Korean student tells her hopefully. *"Not good writer?"*

Vivian senses her fear but is too tired for compassion. "I asked you to type. It says on the syllabus."

Kim continues to look straight at her, though there is something chalky about her gaze, as if a less than average amount of light is going in or coming out. "Oh, yes. Oh, yes. But typewriter of mine–" pausing to let teacher Vivian finish the sentence as she sees fit.

"For next week," says Vivian, "get your typewriter fixed. Or use a computer in the library, okay?," maintaining herself stern but friendly as her words hit against the student's flat, smiling face and come back to her.

Kim scoots out the door. Bad Alex, as she calls the blond boy now, shows her his notebook, in which he has scribbled half an illegible page of his "first draft" of the assignment that, by the way, he really couldn't get into, he doesn't care for personal writing, could she give him a more intellectually challenging topic?

Vivian says with a smile, "I'd say writing about yourself is *inordinately* challenging. I'm ten years older than you and I'm still pretty mysterious to myself," a bit of honesty she hopes will appease the troublesome boy. Bad Alex, however, looks her in the eye for longer than he has to, then turns away abruptly, as if she has somehow shown herself to be unworthy of him.

"FABULOSO! THE ONLY WRITER with vision in English 472! Besides *moi,* of course! Paul, you won't believe this but I was just *thinking* about you!"

Her voice on the phone is as fervently tremulous as he remembers. She has the same number as ten years ago, as if time has somehow snagged and eddied around him and her, turning and turning. His face feels hot.

"You sound great, Jory. You sound terrific."

She laughs her light laugh that used to raise the hairs on his arm. "Things have been marvelous and terrible," she says, hinting at events on the outer reaches of his depth. That's all she'll tell him over the phone. No facts. No credentials, sorry. He remembers her odd impulses, the rules for behavior she'd make up fresh for each new occasion, which made him see her as one of those people fully alive in the self-making. "The rest when you come over," she says, her voice a wisp of sound for him to reinforce in his imagination.

VIVIAN MUST BE A LITTLE ANGRY with Paul or she'd be home now instead of sitting at the office desk which is hers Tuesday and Thursday P.M. She has pushed the other instructors' memos and interdepartmental envelopes to the far corner; bending over the cleared space she reads the essays slowly, allowing the students' experiences, however banal, to afflict her. In general the papers are as error-filled as those of her UIC students, but in subject and treatment a lot less predictable. Here is Bonita Marie Katz's first sexual experience in all the specific, concrete detail she'd asked for last week. *Rubbing against me I could feel his erection like a little doorknob in the middle of his underpants I thought "This has happened because of me!!!"*

Vivian's cheeks redden for these students; she feels tender toward them, toward their transcendence of punctuation, their childish, egotistical courage. Alex the Good's essay is a little verbose but unflinching as he describes how his father abused him mentally and physically. He is comfortable with semicolons; there is nothing to write in his margins but checks.

Kim's, she has saved for last, in part because of the title, "Maggot." It begins with a description of Kim's loneliness in primary school. *I have no friend,* she writes, *until Jin Lee has come,* describing the new girl's crooked teeth, and how people made fun of this new, ugly girl Jin Lee–Kim uses the word ugly–but Kim loved her, and they were best friends in school in Seoul, till the girl's father left and her mother went to live with her brother and his family in another province. Then for years afterward there were no friends in Kim's life–Vivian thinks this is what the essay is saying–for years no friends, in addition to the fact that or perhaps because of the fact that–Vivian has to guess at the transitions–*school is so much hard with my large sister marry, I have wept, I am no good with my books except in arts I am alright ok.*

The concluding paragraph, written in her clear, childlike hand, isn't at all hard to read, but Vivian has to go over it twice. It seems to be a description of the bottom of a garbage pail–a response, perhaps, to her suggestion that they end their essays with an image along with the explanation or summary. Vivian takes one of her contact lenses out, adds a drop of wetting solution, and reads that washing out the big pail one week Kim discovered this fuzz of whiteness at the bottom, and reaching down (why would she reach down, why stick her bare soft child's hand into the bottom of a garbage pail? even sponging her kitchen counter Vivian wears rubber gloves), she brought up for inspection *many, small, white, soft, moving, maggot.* Which somehow–the essay doesn't explain, or else Vivian can't make sense of the explanation–gave her the courage or inspiration or energy to go with her sister and brother-in-law to America.

Vivian feels a bad taste rising up her throat. Had Kim in fact felt tenderness for the disgusting maggot creatures, giving her the inner strength to improve her life? Vivian puts the paper down on the desk. She is sick to her stomach and sick to her brain, certain it was revulsion that Kim had felt, at this visual analogue to her own maggot-like position in her school and community, which a move away would give her a chance to blot out. But the essay seems to suggest the former, although it's badly written enough for ambiguity. The one thing Vivian clearly recognizes in the web of nearly impenetrable inversions and omissions is that Kim will have a lot of trouble passing the course.

JORY LIVES IN A FIRST-FLOOR apartment on a street Paul can't afford; she has always lived, it seems, even when they were students together, a precise financial notch above him. In her foyer, in the light from the open door, she seems physically larger than he remembered–not heavier or taller but more substantial, as if she is made of flesh now instead of precise, exquisite words. Her skin is unlined but her brown hair has threads of gray framing her face with a spider-webby radiance, as she leads him through her dining room into a room with books, plants, a piano. No scatter on the floor of primary-colored objects. No sign, even, of a male presence. "You have so much space here," he says without wistfulness. In her presence he feels beyond self-pity even.

She saw the reviews for the last play of his that showed in town. Good reviews, she says. They were, for the most part. He says to himself with a thrill of joyful despair, *This is the woman I should have married.*

She shows him her book of poetry done by a local feminist press: *Woman on the Back of the Dolphin.* Does he like the title? He does. She doesn't, she says: too portentous. Too something. Today, this moment, she would call the book *Remote Parking*. He smiles as if he understands fully. Perhaps he does understand fully. Her knee is very close to his, although it does not touch. Her husband, she says, has no mind.

He does not ask her, then, why she married him. He enjoys basking in the warmth of his perception that she believes that he, unlike her husband, *has* a mind. When he takes her hand she snatches it back, but several minutes later she puts her hand on the back of his neck, massages a moment, then pulls his face down to hers.

He touches her hair, shoulder, breast. Nowhere, it seems, is off-limits to him. Her presence is a mirror that shows him for the moment young, strong, brilliant, and desirable, desirable because brilliant, brilliant because desirable, and rising into the air with all the terrified ecstasy of a dream of flying.

RUDY ROHNER, the department head, a kind-faced, middle-aged man who walks smilingly with the help of two canes, glances down at the paper Vivian hands him. "Oh dear."

"What," says Vivian.

The man crooks his index finger and presses the knuckle against the inside of one of his eye sockets.

"Bad?" says Vivian.

"She took my remedial course," he says. "Twice. Three years ago and then again last year."

He smiles; Vivian does not. Apparently, although the student has been in the country for eight years, longer than many other nonnative speakers at the Art Institute, she is unable to write English well enough to get her degree. Perhaps another school might graduate her, an art academy, he says. Her artwork, from all reports, is adequate. But the Art Institute offers a B.F.A., which requires an ability to write, say, a comprehensible art history paper. "She works hard," he says. "I passed her, finally, on effort alone. Out of pure compassion."

Vivian is irritated with Dr. Rohner, who exhibits, she thinks, the lazy-minded cynicism of the long-tenured. "I couldn't do that. I'll have her write and rewrite. I'll send her to the writing center."

He shakes his head. "I've seen her struggle for three years. Sometimes her work seems to improve—when she gets a friend or a tutor to go over her draft. But in class, frankly, using just what she has upstairs, her writing is the same as it was when she came here."

"Dr. Rohner," she says, her voice higher than usual from the effort of asserting herself in front of a male superior, "I have trouble accepting that. People get better from practice. Though it takes some longer than others." A B+ student in high school, she believes firmly in the power of work. She has an almost visceral sense of having willed her every achievement.

He picks up one of his canes, taps it on the floor. "I can practice and practice, but I can't run for the bus. Some days I can barely make it to the elevator."

Vivian feels the way she did reading "Maggot." The rubber band that is wrapped around her brain, just tight enough to keep it all together, has begun to hurt.

"I don't mean to sound dismal," he says. "Of course a language problem isn't rheumatoid arthritis. Or maybe it is." He laughs, a series of sharp booms that sounds fake to her. "There's even a name for the problem."

Vivian sits like a student, compelled to listen. If a person who hasn't fully mastered the fundamentals of his own language is suddenly thrust into the situation of having to learn a new language, a process sometimes occurs called *fossilization*. It happens primarily to preteenagers with less than superior IQ's. Language development arrests at the point when the uprooting took place; these children will never be able to learn properly either their own language or any other.

It's as if she has just learned that one of her friends has a terminal illness. "It's horrible," Vivian says.

He nods, though he seems more amused than horrified. "You could pass her anyway," he says.

The suggestion makes Vivian feel even queasier. The only usable bit of information she has gained from the interview is that Kim, the name she has been calling her student, is the student's last name. Her full name, in order, is Jeong Soo Kim. She will call her from now on Jeong Soo.

DRIVING HOME PAUL tells himself that what has just happened is an anomaly, an event like a meteorite that fell into his life with a bright rush that lit up the skies for a moment, then winked out, leaving the world exactly as it was before.

Driving home Paul tells himself that what happened was in a sense, in part, good for his marriage, giving him a large store of pleasure to spend on Vivian and the children like a good family man. Exhilaration radiates around his chest and shoulders, covering past abrasions, armoring him against future damaging people and events.

Then it occurs to him that as a good family man he can never have Jory again, not if he wants to maintain his and Vivian's small store of domestic tranquility. He is suddenly angry with Vivian, whose sexual coolness has in part prompted this misdemeanor, and with his mother, who doted on his father far more than on either of her two kids, and he feels, well, *gypped*–that word belonging to male preadolescence. He is emotionally preadolescent, caught in the worlds of two women for whom he was and is a secondary personage, fit to round out a scene, as Prufrock said, toss off a supporting remark or gesture, but not to command applause, and turning the tight corner into the parking space he rents from a neighbor for forty dollars a month, he scrapes the low wall and bends his fender into his tire so that from now on it will make an unpleasant raspy sound when he turns to the left.

At home the babysitter looks up at him from the couch, mentioning only the date she has with friends tonight; she's glad he's back; has to go home right away and dress.

Unable to look into her eyes he pays her twice what she would ordinarily have earned. "Thank you, Mr. Levine," she says, her warm young voice burning the portals of his ears like sweet poison.

MAKING LOVE WITH PAUL that night, Vivian notes that he is gentler, more attentive to her pleasure than usual, a sign perhaps that the worst between them is over; they will recommence their lives with the sweet, generous intimacy of the time before children. She sets Paul aside as a worry on the wane, one she is relieved not to have to occupy herself with in the face of larger concerns.

In her essay writing class at the School of the Art Institute the two Alexes have solidified their enmity. It is an institution now, a low-level electric current that runs through each class, inactive at times, but capable at any given moment of flaring into nastiness. Alex the Good is the class anathema, more and more isolated in his good intentions, more and more pedantic and arrogant as he feels his intelligent comments dying into the personality morass of the divided classroom. Alex the Bad, on the other hand, has been clever and snide enough to accrue two sidekicks, fresh-faced, weak-willed lads who sit on either side of him and roll their eyes when Alex the Good answers one of her questions. And beside her, Jeong Soo sits up straight in her chair, her flat eyes wide open, at rare intervals making a comment too heavily accented to be understood.

Vivian would like to devote more time to her dissertation, her husband, her children who may grow up delinquent or crazy if they don't get enough of her love. But she must also rethink each week the format for the next class so no nastiness will occur. Moreover, in order to convey her increasingly meticulous understanding of her students' writing weaknesses she must say more in the margins of their papers than they do in the body, comments she will have to explain afterward in individual conferences. And next week when a number of her students, including Jeong Soo, will have their pieces in a show, there is no question she must attend.

She is, she admits to herself, transfixed by the play of energies in this class, as if it somehow mirrors the ebb and flow of her own powers. When the students are receptive or enthusiastic about, say, one of the readings she has assigned, or someone writes an essay strong enough to go over in class, or one of Jeong Soo's eager, halting statements gets a response from another student, Vivian floats home, a good teacher, a worthy human being. But when, as is more often the case, an abyss of silence follows one of her carefully wrought questions, or covert glances among the minions, or a jocular whisper, she comes home too thick-headed to do more than cook for her husband and children as she writes and rewrites in her head the scene she has failed to bring off.

So far, except for a few ecstatic moments, she hasn't found the tack with her class, but she has garnered a lot of wrenching personal information. The girl who looks like a red-headed Glenn Close ran away from home when she was sixteen and got herself addicted to heroin. Stephen White's baby sister was killed last year in a drive-by shooting. Bonita Katz's boyfriend told her he was gay but she thinks he's lying. Far away in Korea, Jeong Soo's mother is ill with something that sounds like cancer. As for the two Alexes, although their lives seem to be relatively unafflicted, they assail her with an eerie string of commonalities. Both have physicist fathers, high school teacher mothers, a single younger brother. Both grew up in a suburb of a large industrial city. In her imagination they are twins separated at birth. Their hostility is Shakespearean, a web of illusion like the false duality of mind and body. If she can reconcile them, she'll be able to unite her own warring parts, create a class in which Jeong Soo Kim and everyone including herself can flourish.

Halfway through the term, Good Alex writes an essay on the

importance of discipline in a child's upbringing. Vivian is impressed; the essay derives from authentic experience, moves spryly from point to point, and contains what seems to her to be a real insight–that a consistent set of rules creates a world in which a young child can find his freedom. This is a paradox she thinks would be useful to examine in the classroom, as many of these students have spent their precollege school days fighting in the name of freedom any means by which authority imposes its will on them. She makes copies for the class and instructs them to follow along as Good Alex reads aloud.

At first the session goes well. The utter silence of respectful absorption soothes and warms her. Alex reads, *My curfew was earlier than that of most of my friends' younger brothers. I fought my father, hating him for it,* and the low murmur of laugh is empathetic. But when Alex goes on to detail his high school achievements, attributable to the fact he had to be home by ten, even on weekends, naming in passing the prestigious Eastern school he'd gotten into (and turned down to come here), there is a hiss from the Bad Alex corner. And when Alex begins his final paragraph, *So there are, as you see, benefits to discipline,* from down the table comes a whisper too loud for Vivian to ignore, "Okay, gee whiz, gol durnit," in which the mockery is unmistakable.

From minion number two, "B and D! You'd never know it, to look at him!"

There's a class hush, a scatter of titters.

Later she will think the teasing might have ended right there if Alex the Good had simply smiled sarcastically and read his last two sentences, which were terse and authoritative. Or if she had taken control, gently chided them, or changed the subject. But now she watches in mild horror as Alex sets his essay down on the table and says without a tinge of self-irony, "I am who I am because of the rules I had to follow. Rules I chafed at, at first. But because of them I know how to get my work done," not angry but so smug that even Vivian is put off. Bad Alex smiles and says quietly, "Chafed at? Oh my. Oh my."

One of his sidekicks adds, squeaking with laughter, "It's the cuffs, Al baby! He's talking about handcuffs! Like they chafe, see?" rubbing his wrists to make his point clearer.

Jeong Soo Kim looks from one to the other, then at her, Vivian, beseechingly, her eyes wide to absorb every difficult American nuance, but the rest of the class is screaming with laughter. Slowly, calmly, as if alone in the room at the end of the period, Alex the Good zips his essay and his books into his backpack and departs.

PAUL HASN'T SEEN JORY since a month ago. She called once but he was vague, and she didn't call again. Now, worn thin by his double resolve—neither to pursue Jory nor confess to Vivian—he is frightened by what he terms Vivian's coolness, imagining it to stem from a love affair she is either involved in or on the exciting verge of. Why else does she spend so much time away from home, and look past him when he tries to talk to her? Not that he entirely blames her. He knows he hasn't been the best companion lately. He isn't righteous so much as afraid of the loss of her, her mind like his so enamored of the sound of words, their ambiguous power.

One Saturday morning when the babies are napping and she

refuses to look up from her book, he tells her the truth about his affair and begs her to do the same.

"I hate you," she says.

He flinches, regathers himself. "Vivian, I'm sorry. It was a mistake. I don't know why I did it. I mean, I do know why I did it and it'll never happen again, but you know– You understand why these things–"

She is glaring at him. He forces himself to look back.

"Look," he says, "you know I haven't felt great about myself lately. These kids have made me neurotic," he says as jocularly as he can. "Not that I didn't already have tendencies–"

"So," she says, "you did it for your mental health?"

"No. Yes." He stares at her helplessly. "But it's over. It happened once only. At least I've been honest."

"Oh, honest! Bully for you!"

"Yes, honest! Which is more than I can say for you. Did you think I was blind, Vivian? Did you think I was so wrapped up in myself I wouldn't notice? But I'd feel better if you came out and told me about it. Nothing could be worse than my imagination."

She steps back away from him. Her arms are crossed. Her eyes are slits, like the eyes of a cat. "Shit."

"Shit? What, Vivian?"

Gazing at him from her distance she seems to have grown immensely large, like a statue of a goddess. She says, "You are so stupid."

"Why am I stupid? How am I?"

She gives him a glance full of loathing, proceeds to her desk in the living room, takes out a sheaf of papers to grade.

"Please, Vivian," he says. "You haven't finished insulting me." His voice holds amusement. He has begun to feel a glimmer of hope.

She runs the point of her red pen back and forth over a corner of her blotter.

"Vivian, you're right, I'm stupid. I need things spelled out for me. Are you in love with someone else?"

She picks up the papers, throws her coat over her arm.

"Vivian, please talk to me. If I'm mistaken I'm relieved. So relieved. I'm crazy about you!"

She pushes past him, shutting the door firmly.

He hears her steps fading but he feels tranquil. His wife is faithful to him. In her fury she looked beautiful to him. One of the babies is crying now and he walks briskly to the nursery, resolved once and for all to do what he must to repair the fabric of this marriage. With his child in his arms he feels enormously hopeful, as if it is simply a matter of will.

VIVIAN DRIVES THE CAR that belongs to her and Paul around and around her block. There is a shining road in her mind down which women are running with determined smiles on their handsome faces. Breaking the circle, she heads down to a city factory district that has been transforming into cafés and loft apartments and gallery spaces.

The exhibit is on the second floor of a building of soot-black brick, from which the letters of the sign *Formfit* are in the process of vanishing. Inside she climbs cracked granite steps through shafts of swirling dust motes to what appears to be a vast empty room, white-bright. She blinks rapidly but she can't see, as if she has stepped out of a cellar into the blazing, shadowless desert.

When her eyes adjust she observes two figures at the far end of the room standing so still they might be some kind of postmodern sculpture. Not far from her a lone woman is bent over what looks like a box on the floor. Her face is inches from it, then she backs slowly away, as if loath to part with it.

Vivian begins her tour in the opposite direction, moving slowly so as not to miss any of her students' names. If she thinks of Paul it's with a small hard shudder, like the coat of a horse twitching off a fly.

Far more interesting is the work of Bonita Katz, lithographs of interlacing male and female forms so black and stark they look like woodcuts; Vivian hadn't expected such direct passion. Stephen White surprises her as well. She'd expected something simple-mindedly provocative from him, the desecration of a sacred polit-ical object or image. But beside his name are three delicate char-coal drawings of birds in flight, loopy and finely shaded. Backing away, admiring how they retain, even so, their essential flight ges-tures, she nearly trips over a rope. On the floor on the other side two arms of bright blue granules spiral out and out from an as-if-swirling center. Except for the color it might be something in the night sky, a star in the process of forming that, bending closer, she discovers to be made up entirely of blue detergent flakes. Titled "Nebula," it is weirdly beautiful. If someone were with her, she would smile at the title and at the name underneath, *Alexander Applebaum,* although she can't remember whether this is the good Alex or the bad.

As she hangs there, the two statue-men come to life and begin to parade the exhibit hall. One is tall, the other short, an odd couple. They amble away from her, pausing to examine this or that piece, murmuring, arguing. She creeps along behind them at their pace, not wanting to overtake them, planning to finish her circuit of the room quickly and depart.

At the last turn she comes upon a group of pieces that stops her. Compared to these, "Nebula" is a clever joke, a good art class answer to a teacher's request to try out new materials. She sees right away what the pieces are made of—cotton, tiny, elongated pearls, black thread, thin twigs—and they suggest things she knows—a nest, a web, a storm cloud, a cocoon, a fly-enwrapped spider—but they seem to be entirely new, on the impossible cusp between imagination and the natural world.

She drops to her knees, examining the largest construction, an airy box made of twigs and black threads woven together. Inside is a wad of cotton that seems to expand as she gazes, oozing out between the black webbing. On various spots on the surface of the cotton there are inroads as from the burrowings of ants, out of which appear to crawl small, white, iridescent shapes that she recognizes as pearls but which, no matter how closely she peers, look exactly as she would imagine, well, maggots. On the card at the base of the construction it reads: *Kim Jeong Soo,* 1992.

She feels bloated, as if her eyes have eaten too much. She squeezes her hands together, trying to make room in her mind for what she is kneeling before, when footsteps assail her.

"Hi there, Miss Vivian," sing out the two men, revealing themselves, blond and dark, stocky and lanky, astonishing in their obvious comaraderie, as her two warring Alexes.

"Gentlemen," she says as coolly as she can. She rises, looks from one to the other. The cold white light blurs their features, their expressions.

"Are you enjoying our feeble creative efforts?" says one of the Alexes.

She wants to ask how they made peace with each other but there is an aura around them that forbids trespass. She says mildly, "There are some good things here."

"Oh, I don't know," says the other, the taller.

"I hope you mean mine," says the short one. They laugh, sharing the joke.

She nods gentle, amused irony, then half strides, half stumbles to her car. An important message, she believes, has been delivered to her. It has something to do with her, with her and Paul, with marriage in general. Something to do with the union of opposites, sarcastic, earnest, male, female, life, death, pearl, maggot.

A really great mind, she has read, is big enough to house two mutually contradictory pieces of information. There is perhaps a language you can speak with someone you love who has betrayed you, a syntax and vocabulary that will let you transcend the fact of the betrayal. But if there is, she has never heard of it; doesn't know how to go about learning it.

She unlocks the door, leans back against the seat, closes her eyes, watching the handsome women runners in her mind who still believe in one step, another step. Ishkebibble, she says to herself. Rumpelstiltskin. Blarghhh.

❦ Mercy ❦

Sometimes in the act of giving pleasure the hinge of my jaw'll catch, and I won't be able to open my mouth all the way. It doesn't happen when I talk or eat. Or yawn. Or get my teeth cleaned. It happens only in the event named above, and it hurts if I force it, and I can't always remember which way last time I wiggled to get free, and I recall instead the two men I saw once and never again, one of whom held my hair with one hand and pounded my face with the other, the side where the hinge of my jaw gets stuck now sometimes, till I was in the car with the door closed shut.

There was no pain. I remember that clearly, though it doesn't improve things. There was just the tiredness, the utter weakness a fish must feel, gills pulsing feebly, pinned by the tail to the floor of the boat.

GINA HAD IT WORSE though, Clark said, to make me feel better. Fifteen men on a beach in Mexico, fog so thick you couldn't see two feet in front. But you could hear her chanting, om om om, low and sweet like blowing into a seashell, Clark said. She was his *friend,* a traveling buddy, that's all–he stresses this. Someone had a gun. When the chanting stopped, Clark stepped toward the silence that had become a hole into which Gina was falling, and the gun waved him back. Get the foock from here, said the gun's bearer, or I blow your brains from your head! Clark, who was to become a professor of Composition and Rhetoric, repressed the impulse to say, It's get the fuck back or I'll blow your brains out. Feeling, among other things, crazy compassion for the guy who'd seen some but not enough American movies. Still the gun was multilingual. When the chanting started again Clark began shaking. Sometimes now, fifteen years later, he dreams his ineptitude, feet caught in cement or quicksand, no strength to save even himself. He wonders if he'll be able to rise to the necessary occasion if it's his lover in danger. Wonders if this is why he's thirty-eight right now with no lover.

WHEN THE MAN who picked us up outside of Binghamton stopped at Goody's Bar and Package Liquor, *I wanna check on my friend,* Lenny and I froze like deer in headlights. It was so late, so moonless dark, so far, still, from where we were heading, that we just held still on the cracked plastic of the front seat, staring out at the blank night beyond the windshield, till the man and his friend stood on opposite sides of the car–bookends, brackets, end-punctuation to our suburban Jewish English-major lives. I'll take shotgun, says the friend, and when Lenny doesn't budge, not from machismo but a failure to access the jargon, he pulls him out of the car. Let's go, Tama, Lenny says, his voice faint as a dog barking across town. But I start moving, I have my arms around my pack and a toe on the ground, about to shift my weight out the door back to my life forever, when the friend jumps in, and the car takes off with my feet sticking out. I feel with a spurt of dread one of my sandals coming off. Start to lose myself in the web of what it might symbolize.

Afterward, in the hotel we found in downtown Binghamton, Lenny told me how, trying to call the police, he forgot 911. It was a crazy thing, his mind was just not working, he had to ask at the 7-Eleven—he cried as he told me.

You don't have to feel guilty, I said generously. I was working on empathy, a step in my personal program of character development, feeling the feelings of the other. I had been a self-centered child, or so it was said. They could have killed you, I said to Lenny. You don't die from rape.

Lenny's guilt kept him up in our muggy hotel room, made him think about taking a martial arts course, about seeing a counselor. It was 1978. Jimmy Carter was in office, though we didn't think about it. Disco screamed through the open window. We went over his responses in depth, from their origin in the American frontier ethic to his relationship with his blustery father.

Hey, thanks, Lenny said. But he looked at me as if I'd become someone else. To help him find his way back to me I described what he'd missed, the looks and personality of the driver's friend, not much older than we were, hard and skinny, with army-short hair the color of his scalp. Who in a book would be named something from the Bible but called by the name of an unattractive minor animal, Mink or Wolverine. Would swear every other word. To me he said over and over, Shut the fuck up. I had no idea I had been talking. I thrashed about, pulled at his fingers, trying to disengage without hurting him, as my mother said to do with my younger sister. Through the hotel window came someone's clear rage: I was better off before I met you!

Lenny said, You could have bitten his arm. Or stuck your fingers in his eyes.

Clearly, he wanted to break up with me.

Have mercy, I said.

The next morning we went back for my sandal—I knew the place more or less, and who'd want one shoe? But though we looked for an hour and found a woman's pointy-toed pump (leather uppers) there was nothing of mine.

MY OLD SOCIALIST LANDLORD, former union baker, was mugged, once, by a group of junior high thugs who not only took his wallet but punched him in the stomach. For no reason. In bed a week, he blamed not the boys but the System (capitalism), which drains out all your human feeling, he said, rolling a piece of generic bread into a finger to dip in the soup I'd brought him: Punks. I pity 'em.

Afterward Gina ran naked into the ocean, said it had passed through without touching her. I am not this body, she said to herself, my sister/alter ego. I've never met her in fact, but part of me aspires to her. A more devout Buddhist than I am a Jew, she has a system large enough to comprise what happened to her. Although her fingers trembled slightly, her face and voice, I imagine, were calm without the comfort of a boyfriend. The assault had failed to reach the radiant core of her.

I gave a pair of policemen the details of my assailants, including tone of voice, texture and smell of skin. I bought a baking powder douche because baking powder cancels refrigerator odors and sounds cleaner than clean, no? But for me, for weeks afterward, though I'd upended my torso for quick and easy entry, it burned when I walked and when I peed, and kissing Lenny wasn't the same either. I used to love to smooch him, on the couch, in the car driving—I loved the smell of him, even when he hadn't brushed his teeth for a while. When school started in the fall we were planning to share an apartment. But afterward, with the pain gone so we could have sex again, we kissed only when he wanted to, not ever from my own impulse.

I think I'm angry, I remember saying.

—With those guys? I don't blame you.

I don't know, I said, and he looked scared to death. I did not pursue the subject.

TO BE SURE, nothing's resolved with "those guys," over whom in my dreams and daytime fantasies I wield the knife of castration. But they aren't only out of reach of my actual vengeance, they're out of my ken, Bad Guys, from nightmares and not daily life—no one I know.

I hugged Lenny. When school started, I studied somewhat harder than before. I did not become pregnant. Lenny and I very slowly became unacquainted. Like those Moslem men who cast out their violated wives and sisters, he felt I should have saved myself. (I might be wrong here.) At this moment I do not know where he is or what he is doing. His degree, I think, was in Psychology.

I switched to European history, which I teach now (Medieval and Renaissance) at a small town branch of a state university. I publish infrequent articles. I'm writing a book about Christian saints. I'm married to a sweet and burly man who teaches social studies and coaches wrestling at the local high school, who'll protect me from marauders on the street. But when a male student cites an opinion with any ruffle of animosity I find it hard to disagree. Now class, who can address what Richard is saying? The area in which I feel utterly safe from harm is small, and under assault not only from people like the "guys" but something Lenny said a night or so after the event, Tell me the truth, was there any...pleasure?, a little embarrassed. But he just had to know.

I want to beat on him—I think about that. To sock him in the mouth, the eye, watch it turn dark the next day. What kind of pleasure? I'll scream. Is there pleasure for *you* being one hundred percent at someone's mercy?

THERE WAS NOTHING but terror in the event—I've gone over it looking for nuances, with friends, shrinks, and now husband Dan, though he's not big on nuances. He doesn't find power erotic at either pole. The sort of thinking that mixes good and evil he finds "sick." I sleep well in the absoluteness of his distinctions. And that he does not require fellatio. When I do it as a favor he seems to appreciate it.

Still, there's that weird boy at our son's summer camp, not so big himself, who likes to play with the little kids, the preschoolers, Mercy, it's called. In this game you take someone's thin wrist in your two hands and twist in opposite directions till the fragile chains of cells pull away from each other with a sensation that feels partly like ripping and partly like burning. It's supposed to stop when the victim yells Mercy! or maybe just a little later, this game of machismo, of personal grit in the face of pain, good practice, perhaps, for dissidents of repressive regimes who will not betray their comrades. But when I go to pick Noah up in the gym where the children wait for their rides, the weird kid is holding his arm, and Noah, who rarely cries from physical pain, has this blank look, as if the world has just opened its horrendous possibilities. What do you think you're doing! I hiss at the boy, and he puts his fingers in his ears. I hold him by the shoulders: If you ever touch him again, do you hear me? if you put another hand on my son, I'm coming for you, do you hear what I'm saying? you think you know about pain but that's nothing compared to what I'll do to you!

Big talk. It bounces off his skull of some weird, impermeable fusion of lead, kryptonite, and pure evil. He twists his fingers deeper in his ears, shuts his eyes. I give him a shake, not as hard as I'd like, in truth I want to kill this boy for making the world one shade darker for my child so full of light. This is a bad kid, I say to myself, with, obviously, problems at home. He has trouble controlling him-self, the director says, seating him in a corner to wait for his mother who hasn't brought him up properly, as I turn to hide the fact of my shaking, from him, this sick child who'll shoot from towers if he doesn't get therapy soon and maybe even if he does, this demon boy from whom I must save my boy so utterly different from him.

But the next day when I poke my head in the door Noah is with him again. The two spring apart with identical expressions of rapturous guilt, as if caught in some complicit, consensual lovemaking.

IN PAIN THERE IS, or so I recall from childhood, a sexual element. I used to draw Prometheus on his rock, belly open to the beak and talons of Zeus's avenging vulture, Joan at the stake, flames lapping the hem of her tattered dress (crayoned brown to resemble a sack). I had a teacher who asked our class once, seriously, Is there anything you'd give up your life for? I loved this teacher. My sister and I played spy and counterspy, one or the other being captured by the Russians. Confess! she'd scream: Would you rather be Red or Dead? further compressing my hand in the vise on my father's basement workbench. I remember a dark ecstatic quiver, not the sole province of male children.

The old pain/pleasure thing. Aside from God, that's the heart of it, and maybe even as big as God, at least people cry Jesus, cry Satan with the same blood urgency, seeking the pleasure of pain in hope of the same—we need a German word here—Ultimate-idea-feeling-of-light. I knew it once better than I do now, having set it down somewhere or stashed it in some inner pocket, incongruent with the work of becoming a grown-up citizen human being, what people do to keep their livers intact.

But in Roman Empire days, Julitta, a new Christian, saw her

child murdered by a government official and rejoiced in his martyr's death. It's part legend, part fact: inextricable. Julitta is wealthy, noble, running from the Imperial law. Her son Cyricus, three, grown close to her body and soul over two years of hiding and wandering, bites the governor who took him from her, who hurls him off his lap and down steps the way you throw off a pesky kitten. The steps are marble, no doubt, sans carpet. Julitta, rhapsodic in the Christian death of her toddler martyr, goes serenely to her own, which will be accompanied by torture. Mother and son saints, Julitta and little Cyricus.

It was 304 (date substantiated), with Diocletian immersed in the Christian Problem when he should have been securing his borders. More than the Huns he feared monotheism, the laser force of the One God overwhelming the wild crackling Olympian bonfire. But what is this drive to cast oneself into the bonfire? In Alexandria a Christian grandmother named Apollonia is beaten by members of an anti-Christian mob. Some of her teeth fall out. Renounce! someone cries, or it's the pyre for you! But when they light it, she walks in of her own free will: Saint Apollonia.

With young Christian girls—virgins—sainthood was harder to come by. Moved perhaps by their youth or the beauty of a face, officials promised them their lives and more if they returned to the Imperial fold, sacrificed to Minerva, married a noble. Catherine is my favorite, highborn, beautiful, and learned. Denying her faith she can marry the Emperor. Both she rejects, instead converting fifty philosophers hired to best her in debate along with the Empress she was to supplant. There are no documents to support any of these tales, but they inspired Medieval Christians including

Joan of Arc. Beaten and left to die in prison, Saint Catherine is fed by a dove. The spiked wheel designed to end her life in torment falls to pieces as she's bound to it, its spikes injuring several spectators. She bends her head to the block, calling down blessings on those who'll remember her, ecstatic, mirroring the agony of Christ. Milk flows from her severed veins and arteries. The instrument of torture that failed to harm her will be called the Catherine wheel.

But at dusk when a tree or stop sign turns into the figure of a man, I can't rise on the wings of her unimaginable suffering or ecstasy. Nor, in my self-defense class, can I strike the padded attacker with even half my strength. My blows have an element of caress. I am neither saint nor self-protector. My ego refuses either to die or prevail.

Don't think so much, says my instructor, herself a rape victim turned fierce with her message. You have the power to save your life.

—I know that in theory.

You don't have to be a saint, says Dan.

—If I were a saint I'd have forgiven them.

There's no need to forgive them. They're scum, Dan says.

—That's what makes it so hard.

IT'S WHAT SEPARATES the Medieval mind from that of the Renaissance, I tell my students, the notion of there being two sides. It's the perspective from the mountaintop. Good-hearted, inept Jimmy Carter. What removes us from Catherine on one side and the Huns on the other, a sense of the unresolvable ambiguity of practically everything. I bear it like an illness.

My personal Huns had no such interior division. Resolute and fierce they followed the rush of their blood to its culmination in act. If their minds held a self-image, it wasn't even as naughty-boy but executor of a primitive justice. The younger, the Wolverine, kept calling me whore, as if rape were a punishment he was meting out for my promiscuity. Cornell–the name on my sweatshirt–'s a real cathouse!, he kept saying that. He went first, and after waiting patiently for his friend, slightly paunchy, limper of dick, to finish, he re-unzipped and said he wanted to do it again, not in the car but on the cool night asphalt of the empty lot we were parked in, and this time I was to show how much I liked it.

Sometimes now I stop my car in bad neighborhoods, buy a Coke from a store outside of which dissolute teens stand trying to get up the energy to mug someone. As if this fifteen-year-old event is my primal scene, to be played and replayed till it comes out right or else covers over what in fact occurred, what I haven't detailed yet, not even to Dan.

But fifteen years ago my jaw was starting to hurt, something like a molar toothache, an augmenting pain with no end in sight. Then in the face of Wolverine's uncircumcised dick, his bullet-shaped, almost hairless head, I push panic to one sector. From the small area of mind that can still think and speak come words from some high school play, nauseous sticky-sweet in the back of my throat: You are a *kind* man. You are a good and *merciful* man. Not to Wolverine but to the older, limper one. Prone on his backseat, I half raise my head, palms together in the Christian prayer position, though there's nothing Christian in what I am doing, no ideal to exalt, of faith or sexual purity, no one's life to save besides my own.

I speak into his eyes, beseeching like Olive Oyl, like Pauline tied to the tracks: I've learned my lesson. I don't need to be hurt anymore, please, really I don't.

Kiss my hand, he says.

I do so.

Kiss my dick, says Wolverine.

I reach, but clumsily. He pulls back the flap of gentile skin.

—Kiss it I said!

I'm about to comply when limp-dick grabs his buddy by the back of his jacket. Stop farting around.

Keep your eyes off the plates, says Wolverine. One look back and we're coming for you!

Thank you, I say, once, so as not to seem ironic.

But I do not feel ironic. I feel unambiguous gratitude, for the moment at least. Later I'll hate them for rubbing my face in the smallness and smarminess of my female power. But there on the pebbly asphalt of the parking lot I tremble with love for the paunchy one for holding off his friend. He stands at the back of his car with his arms crossed like a genie from a bottle, like my hero-deliverer, my God in his mercy.

I'd rather be Red than Dead, I say to myself. I'd rather be anything than dead. I limp in my one shoe away down the road.

❦ If You Step on a Crack ❦

H er first and only husband sat on the couch in front of the pre-game interview. From four doors south across Waveland Avenue the lights of Wrigley Field cast their salmon glow on his long-sleeved shirt. Three stories down, the steps of Cubs and Cardinals fans crunched along the alley, overlaid by spates of mild, ritualized jeering. Blue and red caps bobbed toward the bleacher entrance. "Come, let's cheer them on to ignominy," said Andy, to whom she had been married longer than any of her friends to their husbands. He held out his hand.

She'd been watching a golden-haired boy of twenty or so take a whizz in the alley. "What fun," she said, to either, to both.

He laughed. "You have to think like a Cubs fan. It's not victory we're after. It's watching them play almost well enough to win, then making fun of them and yourself for getting sucked in to hop-ing!" He laughed again, as if this were the first time he'd said this. A high school vice principal, he was in his heart the Cubs play-by-play man. He'd call the games just ahead of Brennaman and Harry Caray with patter at times identical to theirs.

"That's my back door," she called out the window. "Why don't you go smell up your own neighborhood?"

The boy turned up a face hauntingly beautiful in the manufactured twilight. "Wanna zip me up, lady?"

"I'm calling the police!"

"Like I'm scared," he said.

"I'm boiling the oil," she shouted, "so why don't you stay right there under my window with your thing hanging out–"

"Maya," Andy said, "he's a Cardinals fan. That's how they're raised in St. Louis."

She turned, saw her five-year-old twins at the doorway, their identical mouths open in the same little O. "Guys, come here, I want to show you what not to turn into."

"Maya."

"I want to help speed you to an early death in which your body parts erode slowly," she whispered into the dusk. Her sons were dancing on tiptoe at her elbow, her husband was massaging the back of her neck, but she felt alone on an island. Last week at the mammogram follow-up she'd read upside down the last line of a paragraph on the printout on Ahranjani's desk: *The possibility of tumor cannot be ruled out.* She'd asked him, coolly, she thought:

–What are the chances either way?

–Fifty-fifty, I'd say. The calcifications bother me.

–Why do they bother you?

–They don't follow the line of the vein.

–But *calcifications*... They sound so *innocent!*

–Maya, get hold of yourself.

At the door of Andy's study trying to recall the tremor or whatever it was in her voice that Ahranjani had responded to, she'd felt her knees go weak. But Andy had processed the information so quickly she wasn't sure he'd absorbed it. "Fifty-fifty? Well, we'll think about the good fifty!"

She hadn't wanted to distress him. She'd wanted to bear her apprehension with grace and courage. But his optimism seemed as empty and vague as a sound bite.

"Maya, honey, you'll know tomorrow. The worst part's the uncertainty."

"*I'*ll know?" she had said, the words coming from between her teeth. "What do you mean *I'*ll know? Am I the only one who'll know?"

"Of course I'll know too," he said, more confused than wounded.

She did not say that the worst part was not at all the uncertainty but the chance of pain and disfigurement and early death. Her friend Gail, four years younger, had just had a lumpectomy. Her aunt had died from something that started with a bad mammogram. Her childhood heroine had been Edith Cavell, the English nurse and member of the anti-German underground who, facing the firing squad, had refused a blindfold. Maya imagined Edith with her back to the bloody wall, a corner of her gray cotton gown rippling in the wind, her open eyes boring deep into the mouths of the muskets that would end her life. But she didn't want to be Edith Cavell. She didn't want to be caught and shot. "Let's make water balloons," she said to Max and Alex. "When the enemy comes we have to be ready."

. . .

BECAUSE NOW everything meant something.

It was like twenty years ago when she swallowed a whole tab of acid when everyone else was doing half and got stuck in that quivery space right after the luminous ascent. Objects unfurled and refurled, into and out of whatever they were made of, threatening to freeze at the point of terrifying ugliness. Then, it had been dangerous to speak with friends you didn't absolutely trust or to look too long at your face in the mirror. Now, for the past week, she ate only brown rice and vegetables high in vitamins A and C. She watched films from the forties with their classic, unambiguous lines of comedy or heroism. She tried to visualize the troops of her white blood cells marshaling their protective force at given parts of her body. But still the part of her mind attempting control could not fully manage itself. She saw herself bald and then weak, sick, dead, mourned for–Andy bereft, then marrying again, Max and Alex confused by her absence, then used to it, till she was a fragment of memory only a shrink could call up, a sweet, blurry face in a photograph.

Twenty years ago before husband, children, house, job, tripping on daredevil acid in women's lockup she had kept panic in check by meditating on the worst life could present her–poverty, shame, imprisonment for up to five years (the maximum penalty for possession of a shopping bag full of marijuana). She'd imagined herself on a park bench, sans family and friends, a filthy blanket, a few torn paperbacks–all she owned–in a bag at her feet, and her mind, infused with the Zen she'd been practicing those days, had, gasping, managed to say, I can take it! When her boyfriend's family's lawyer came to lower her bond she was calm and remote, amused, almost, which annoyed, she could see, even her boyfriend.

But now, tonight, testing each possible downward step in her current potential tragedy to see if it could bear her weight, she couldn't get as far, even, as "bald." She couldn't embrace for a minute the vision of her hair falling out, not one coarse, wavy red strand. So although she had come to the point as a Cubs fan of being able to recognize Andre Dawson on the street and to impress her husband's friends with her recall of, say, the number of home runs he'd hit his first year as a Cub (49), she couldn't watch the Cubs on TV with Andy tonight. If she stepped on a crack she'd break her mother's back. When someone peed on their aluminum siding it eroded her small store of good luck. If the Chicago Cubs lost to the St. Louis Cardinals tonight, her body's immune system would be overwhelmed, her T-cells helpless in the face of the dark area in the X-ray of her right breast, a spot that was to be removed tomorrow morning and biopsied. And the Cubs were a game below five hundred, their hitting the second worst in baseball.

HER SISTER CALLED. "Maya," she said, "I had *three* and they were all negative!" Her voice was loud and bright, thrumming with her own medical good fortune.

"I know," Maya said.

"You sound on top of it," her sister said. "I was a basket case the first time. I kept thinking about—you know. The last time wasn't so great either, I thought three strikes and you're out—"

"Call no man happy till he be dead," Maya said. "Sophocles said that. Or was it Aeschylus?"

"You're showing off, Maya."

"Janice," she said, "I have to put the kids to bed."

"Frankly," Janice said cheerfully, "I think it's just a matter of time. Sometimes I think I should get a *preventive* mastectomy."

"Janice, the kids are screaming for me."

"JANICE DRIVES ME CRAZY," she said to Andy.

"Me too," he said, laughing as if he knew just what she meant. She felt none of the flow of warmth that signaled that she believed he did know.

He leaned back against the couch and stretched his legs as the Rainbow Children's Choir, all of whom had a physical or mental handicap, sang the national anthem. Her children sat on the floor with their backs to the screen, working on their Lego constructions. Max's were always closed, perfect boxes, while Alex made vehicles bristling with flags and weapons. "The Star-Spangled Banner" rose swirling, pure and shrill into the air of the TV room. "Look, Mom," one of the boys would say from time to time, thrusting a primary-colored artifact into her hands. "Oh dear," she'd say, "will it explode?" Or, "I'd feel so safe inside!" relieved to see by their expressions of pleasure that she had not inadvertently conveyed her self-concern.

Once, the sound of crunch signaled footsteps in the alley. She and the boys leaned out the window, giggling frantically, juggling the wobbly balloons they'd filled with water. But so far no one else had tried to urinate. "It's a beautiful night here at Wrigley Field," Andy said.

"It's a beautiful night," said Harry Caray, "as the Cubs fight to hold onto fourth place."

HER PARENTS CALLED as they always did at eight on Sunday. "It's raining here," her father said, his voice full of significance like a TV weatherman.

Her mother clicked on. "Maya, we got you! You're never home! Did he tell you, we started the grill and then the heavens opened up? I stood out there holding an umbrella over his head, we should have had a picture but the salmon was terrific, I wish you'd been here. Oh, and by the way your father is just a little angry with you. There's only one grandma left and how many birthdays is she going to have?"

"Hey," her father said to her mother, "don't put it on me."

"Oh dear," Maya said. "I'm sorry."

"It's *your* mother, Irving," her mother said.

Her parents' voices were a waterfall in which she stood breathing shallowly. Tomorrow's surgical procedure was one of a number of things she couldn't tell them about, including her long ago drug arrest, the theft of her purse at gunpoint, and something Alex had said to his teacher at school.

"Don't be upset, Maya," her father said. "If you call tomorrow she'll understand."

"She probably doesn't even remember," her mother said.

"I'll call her tomorrow." Her lips were curved in the small firm smile of Edith Cavell before the firing squad. "Bye. I love you."

. . .

BY THE TIME THE CHILDREN'S lights were out it was the top of the third, and the Cubs were already two down. She thumbed through the paper on the kitchen table, gazed at the first of the four words to unjumble on the Dear Abby/mindgame page—FLONE. She tried *elfon; fenol;* arrived at *felon,* stared till it too looked wrong. She wandered from room to room, adjusting pillows, returning small bright plastic figures to bright plastic tubs. She settled across the sofa from Andy, stretching her bare feet toward his lap.

He began to massage the arch of her foot, kneading deliciously just short of pain. He slipped a finger between two of her toes, a gesture as exquisitely sexual as junior high school, that sometimes liquefied the lower half of her body. But now her skin felt numb to the sixth or seventh layer. On the screen the Cubs pitcher walked two men in a row. His next pitch was so low the catcher collapsed on it, searched for it under his knees as the men went to second and third. "Ball three low," Andy said. "Wilkins picked it out of the dirt. I think Morgan's losing it."

"Wilkins made a great stop," said Harry Caray. "Looks like Morgan's having a little control problem."

Maya sat with her foot on her husband's lap, gauging the depth and the parameters of her isolation. It had been there last year at the cabin they rented in Door County, amid the pines, the mosquito repellent, Andy and the boys' obvious joy. It had been there the year before over expensive food at the Drake on their fifteenth wedding anniversary. In their current lovemaking she sometimes counted her husband's eyes one, two, three, four, or rode into orgasm on a fantasy of cinema and leather in which he played no part.

She returned to the kitchen, unscrambled the rest of the words without a pause, STORN (snort), DAWTOR (toward), SPOCER (corpse), angry with the *Jumble* editors for that last word. She stuffed the paper in the wastebasket.

There had once been between her and Andy something that could stop her thought. She remembered an airport good-bye, and tears in his eyes as he bent to pick up his suitcase. And the taste of his breath, the light prickle of the hairs on his arms; the entire week of his absence she slept with her cheek to the T-shirt he'd left at her apartment. When she'd had the twins at thirty-eight she had started to believe all over again that nothing was too late, there was nothing they couldn't have if they worked hard enough. But the euphoria was gone, and that sense of visceral, passionate connection so remote it was less a feeling than a remembered idea—not through anyone's viciousness, just the normal erosion of intensity over time. If things turned out well tomorrow she would be happy, and perhaps happy with Andy, but some time not very far away, she felt sure, they would separate.

THE CUBS TIED IT UP in the bottom of the third, and Maya returned to the TV room. Andy held out his arms. She sat down beside him.

"Feeling better?" he said.

Blandly handsome Ryne Sandberg, who'd just gotten a double, took a step out from the base. In the on-deck circle Andre Dawson swung three bats around and around his head. Mark Grace, who looked like a new U.S. Marine, grounded out to the pitcher. "I'm trying not to think about it," she said.

He nodded approval. "For the best."

A flash of white streaked before her eyes. She said in a light, conversational voice that hurt her ears, "You know, the real problem with illness and death is how alone you are."

"Maya," he said, "I do not believe you're ill. In fact, you look terrific tonight."

The sexual desire in his voice made something harsh rise to the back of her throat. "I'm trying to behave," she said. "I don't seem to be doing very well."

"You're doing fine," he said. She folded her hands in her lap, watched Dawson fly out to end the inning.

"This is how it's been," Andy said. "They are just not executing!"

"They look tuckered out," Harry Caray said cheerfully. Steve Stone said, "They look bored. For a composite forty-three million you'd think they'd put out a little!"

To ease her sudden, irrational anger, which filled the air around her head with a kind of black dust, she tried to direct her breath in one nostril and out the other, a meditation she'd last practiced with her legs crossed on the bare metal bunk in women's lockup. But she hadn't done anything like this in twenty years; she was assailed by the image of herself in a beauty chair, asking the operator, please, to weave the long thick curls she was shaving from her head into a wig that wouldn't look like a wig. Wearing the imaginary cunningly fashioned natural-hair wig that still looked like a wig, she saw the shock in the eyes of her friends as they said words of admiration or consolation and turned away, just as she had turned away from the blue cotton-knit turban her friend Gail had worn over her own balding head. Blue is restorative.

Unable to erase or alter the mental picture, she worked to embrace it. Envisioned her face without the mane of hair that even now, in her forties, strangers would comment on. Imagined her features *sans* the aureole of her hair, small and ordinary-looking below the chemotherapy turban. Imagined her hair growing back under the turban, thicker and curlier than before, just as her aunt's had, miraculously, without a trace of gray; in her coffin she had looked young and tragically beautiful, like Snow White. Standing before the firing squad, Edith Cavell had shaken her head at the proffered blindfold. Maya said the word "brave" to herself, a cup of tea to hold in her hands. Andy sat with his arm stretched out toward her on the back of the couch. Shyly, almost, he touched her shoulder. She inhaled through her left nostril, observed the stream of air passing out through her right, though her breaths were coming so hard her throat hurt trying to slow them down. "I keep thinking about my aunt," she said.

He lowered the volume on the set. "That was a long time ago. Detection is better now."

"I can't remember what they called the bad stuff on her X-ray. Was it calcifications?"

"Maya, you're going to drive yourself crazy."

"Do you want me to read Norman Cousins?"

"I don't know!"

She picked up one of the water balloons that were laid out on a towel under the window. She jiggled it in her hand. "The problem," she said, "is you have no capacity for flash-forward."

"Would you like to make love?"

"No!" Her voice was pure and high to her ears, soundless as a dog whistle. "I would like to throw this water balloon at you!"

"Go ahead," he said.

"That's the problem."

"What? That I won't fight with you?"

"You skitter over the surface of things. Your feelings have no substance." She shifted the heavy balloon from hand to hand, a little bomb; a breast. Within such frail walls its unexpected weight made it seem surreal, as if it had come from a place with laws different from hers.

"Maya," he said, "I know why you're doing this."

He explained that she, like most people, revised history in the light of present good or bad fortune. If you're happy, then everything that's ever happened seems a rung in the ladder that has brought you there; and vice versa. "Mostly you like me, Maya. Try to remember that."

"Jesus," she almost shouted, "don't go rational on me! If I disappeared, you'd grieve for a day, then onward."

"That's idiotic!"

Her throat hurt where the words had emerged but there was more to say. "If someone accosted me on the street, you'd smile politely. You'd say, I wish you'd stop that, young man."

She squeezed the balloon, daring it to burst. "I hate Norman Cousins," she said more lightly. "How can you tell someone to lower stress? Doesn't it create stress, working to lower stress?"

When she looked up, his face had gone rubber. As if she had said something in English that turned out to be, in the local language, an obscenity.

. . .

SHE OPENED THE REFRIGERATOR, gazed at the covered bowls, the row of clean-wiped condiments in the door compartment.

She walked into the living room, raised the blind, gazed out on the dark garden. A roar from the crowd came in the window, crescendoed, stopped abruptly, a long fly ball caught on the warning track or rocketed into the stands just below the foul pole.

She ran down the hall to the children's partially open door, her eyes following the crack of hall light across Alex's blanket. She tiptoed into the room, lay down on the floor beside his futon. He breathed softly, evenly, in and out. His neck smelled sweet.

She returned to the living room. Outside, the pink-purple air hummed with the sounds of Wrigley Field, the rise and fall of fan pleasures and disappointments, a net of normality to catch her if she fell. She raised the screen, leaned out as far as she could, drinking in the warm, noisy summer air. If she believed in God, she might have resorted to bargaining: Give me good news tomorrow, and I'll plant an acre of trees in Israel, I'll give a tenth of my income to the Jewish United Fund. But her offer, she was sure, was too paltry and trite for a God with real power over life and death, and even if the Eternal would have agreed to such a specifically Jewish, unimaginative pledge, she would have had to preface it with, "Excuse me, I know you haven't heard from me in a while, and I know it's wrong to come to you just when I need something, and I'm not sure even now, talking, if someone is listening out there," her words dying into the silence of embarrassment and shyness.

"Don't jump," Andy said.

She pulled her head in, turned politely around.

"You were awful to me," he said.

"I know. I'm sorry." Although close enough to touch, he seemed small to her, as if she were looking at him through the wrong end of a telescope. "I don't think I love you, Andy."

"You don't mean that."

She fixed on the fine black mesh of the screen above the open mouth of the window, wanting to suck her words back into wherever they had come from. As a teenager her first uttered *I love you* had made something like flowers leap from her skin, melded the jumble of joy and terror and weakness in her limbs into a single emotion that felt eternal. Certain words, she had always known, had an alchemical creative force. She gave him a look of terrified apology.

"It's not true," he said. "Why do you say it if it's not true?"

Her eyes bored into his eyes, she cocked her head to the same side and at the same angle as his, trying to become better than she was. "I'm a bad yogi. I can't make the journey all by myself to the end of pain."

He embraced her, kissed her neck, kissed down the top of her chest to where her bra began.

"Here's a Zen story," she said. "A monk is being chased by a tiger to the edge of a cliff. He starts to climb down the cliff, but there's another tiger below, looking up hungrily. As the ledge he's on starts to crumble he sees a flower growing out of a rock, and smiles at the flower. And receives instantaneous and perfect enlightenment."

"And so?"

"I don't feel like smiling at flowers."

"Maybe you need more tigers in your life."

He unhooked her bra, kissed a circle around her right, her questionable breast.

He said, "Don't you want me to do this?"

She wanted to want him to do this, perhaps their last lovemaking with her body intact. But the idea made her shudder. Her skin was a layer of dead whitish cells, dry and tight over her bones; she could not suffer the opening and entry into her body like Edith Cavell. She turned to one side, shielding her chest with her upper arm. "Okay," he said. "All right."

He returned to the TV room. She walked downstairs, out to the front gate. South across Waveland the heads of the top row of bleacher fans bobbed and swayed against the purple sky. Behind her their own white-sided building glowed a ghostly amethyst, insubstantial as a storybook house. The air shimmered with the silence of a mass of people waiting for something to happen. There came a loud cheer; someone had done something good. But lots of Cardinals fans had come to the game. She couldn't see the scoreboard, didn't know whether to be pleased or concerned.

The wind rose slightly, a cool September breeze. Turning to go back in, she saw at her feet, glowing salmon-pink like everything else, a crumpled McDonald's carryout bag. Inside were the remains of a Big Mac and an empty Batman cup, recently tossed over the chain-link fence that encircled their yard. Holding the bag between thumb and forefinger she felt her way along the narrow passage between her house and a neighbor's, unlocked the wooden gate to the alley.

She had just dropped the bag into one of the alley trash bins when footsteps she hadn't registered made her aware of them as they abruptly ceased. Less than ten feet away a man stood with his back to her. She watched a dark spot form between his legs at the base of her house. A puddle gathered at his feet. He danced out of the way, resnapping his pants, giving her a smile of somewhat inebriated complicity. Blond, with small, exquisite features, he might have been the man she had screamed at earlier that night.

"You seem to like our facilities," she said.

He gazed at her, his smile drying on his face. He shrugged and walked away. She stared at his retreating back, the triangular narrowing from shoulder to hip of a well-built young man. She called out, "You know, you're not that well hung."

He stopped, turned. "What's that, Ma'am?"

"Did your mother bring you up to be a disgusting pig? Where are your manners and your brains?"

"Shit," he said.

She stood her ground, inured to pain like a yogi, like someone who knows no matter what that she will die tomorrow. "You have an itsy-bitsy teeny-weeny dick. I want you to think about that next time you want to pull your pants down where you're not supposed to. What, are you going to sock me? There's a brave lad."

He took a step toward her, a hand upraised. His handsome boyish face looked red, though it might have been the lights of Wrigley. Part of her wanted to run but her legs were stiff; she didn't move even when he was close enough for her to smell the beer on his breath. But when he grabbed her shoulder so hard the little bones crunched together, she was astonished to find herself doing what had been forbidden so many years ago she couldn't remember ever having had the impulse: she bit the back of his hand. As he fell back, drawing his hurt hand to his mouth, she felt on her tongue the little hairs on his skin, the oddly metallic taste of his blood, and she fled inside the gate and upstairs, locking doors.

From the TV-room window she and Andy tossed out water balloons, watched the young man vanish into the shadows at the end of the alley. They gave each other a high five. She was trembling, he, unnerved by what she had just done, laughing wildly. He put his arms around her; they sank to the floor. She looked at his face, wondering whether or not she honestly wanted to kiss him, when a small, blurred but unmistakeable jolt ran through her body along her spine to the bones of her skull. It was the physical equivalent of a dream she sometimes had of falling out of bed. She jumped up, noticing that one of the children's Lego constructions had fallen off its shelf. Andy shouted out the window, "Stop that!" She felt another jolt. The TV rocked on its stand. "It's your friend," he said.

Down in the alley an old white convertible backed up three or four feet till it banged the garage on the other side. In the driver's seat was a blond-haired, red-faced, handsome young man. Head down, shoulders hunched like a football player, he slammed his car at a corner of their building. There was a distinct crack.

"Our back gate," he said.

In the purple light the man's wet hair looked pink, his head smaller than before. He backed up again. She dialed 911, but as she gave their address she was thrown to the floor. "Andy honey, he's trying to knock our house down!"

"We should have built out of brick," he said.

"That's really funny."

"We're taking things into our own hands," he said, raising the window as high as it would go. He took out the screen. "Let's hear it for Bernard Goetz. Give me a hand with the TV, darling."

Together they lifted the heavy set to the windowsill, balancing it on the edge. "When he makes his next move, just let go," he said. "Let's hear it for Bernard and Mrs. Goetz. Your Honor, Sir, I was protecting my family. Aim for the windshield. I hope we don't kill him."

"Andy, are you sure you want to take the chance—"

Her words trailed off. She stood at the window beside him, burning with a fury so pure and unfettered it was almost love, the two of them, husband and wife together holding their relatively new twenty-four-inch Sony portable television set against the ravaging hordes. There was a siren, a flashing blue light. Startled, she let go of her side of the load. To compensate, Andy pulled back on his side, then to stop the set from falling on him, he sent it forward and out the window. It dented the trunk of the big white car speeding off down the alley, then smashed into its elemental shards of glass and pressboard.

The police car screamed away after the convertible and for a moment there was silence. Then came a roar, at first tentative, then crescendoing, sustaining itself. They ran to the living room, turned on the radio to learn that Mark Grace had just crossed the plate. He had blasted a ball out onto Waveland Avenue. With a man on. Bottom of the seventh, Cubs 4, Cardinals 2.

She sat down on the floor beside Andy, leaning back against the sofa. "The floor feels sloped. Does it feel sloped to you?"

"It's always been sloped."

"We should inspect." She tried to get up.

"Tomorrow."

"I'm busy tomorrow," she said. "That's supposed to be funny!"

She broke away from him, saw tears in his eyes, sat down. "What's the matter, Andy? The Cubs might win this one."

He kissed her forehead.

"Andy," she said, "tell me why you're crying."

He wouldn't look at her.

"Andy," she said, "I know why."

He took her hand, kissed it. His cheeks were damp.

"This is what I wanted." She kissed his mouth. Her lips felt warm and larger than usual, she loved kissing him. "To know you're in this too."

"Of course, I'm in it!" he said. "Where else have I been?!"

"But now I *feel* it. Before, I couldn't feel it."

"I don't see why you couldn't feel it!"

He seemed a little angry with her but she was kissing his face, his hands. They made love on the floor like teenagers, wild and mindless of consequences. When at last they rolled onto their separate backs on the rug, he said, "So from now on I can only have you when there's a war going on outside?"

"If you fought to defend your family."

"I don't know if I can take it." He laid his head against the base of the sofa, gazing out at the salmon-gray night.

"You'd better," she said. She watched him absorb the top of the ninth. There was one out. According to Steve Stone, Assenmacher (four saves) was keeping the ball low. "You'd better," she said, but without urgency. The voices of the announcers seemed preternaturally sharp, almost luminous. Balls crackled like lightning into the catcher's mitt. She felt whole, well, immortal as a teenager. "I have this nice feeling," she said, her lips to the top of his arm.

"It'll go away," he said.

"But it's here now," she said, licking his arm, savoring the sharp, sour taste of salt.

❁ Milk ❁

The babies are stirring. You can't not hear it in this house without rooms—cloth scraping cloth, a few grunts too close together to be accident. Then scratching. For some reason when they wake up in the morning they start clawing the crib sheet like little cats. It makes me think, did I leave their nails too long? Or is it instinct—they're digging out into the light like moles or gophers.

"Moles don't dig out," Kevin says. "Moles dig down in. They like it dark, not light. They spend so much time in the ground they don't need their eyes to see anymore. As in 'blind as a mole.'"

"No one says 'blind as a mole.'"

Behind the screen on the far side of the loft one of the boys starts talking to himself—aaooaaooaaoouuaaa—light sweet vowel sounds, as if something nice has just happened and he's reliving it. Kevin burrows like a mole under his pillow.

We have twins, six months old, and they've affected his mind, he thinks. His music. Even when he's alone in the soundproof basement where he writes he can't hear notes in his head because in back of the quiet are babies crying. When he goes to sleep at night—and it's quiet here, just the crickets, the wind blowing, rain sometime—she can't sleep because babies are crying. Babies aren't crying—I get them at the first peep—but he hears them in the wind, the rain, my breathing, his breathing.

"It'll get better," I say to his pillow. "Everybody says."

"Right, in eighteen years when they go away to college. Not that I can afford to send them to college. I'll help them look for a nice apartment in St. Paul, that's what I'll do."

"There are returns now," I say. "They respond to you. They look happy when you walk in the room."

"So does my dog," he says.

"You don't have a dog."

"Right. I hate dogs."

Kevin is pleased with the something clever he finds in that remark. I can still save us, charm him into loving me and the babies. I kiss his neck, run a hand down his hip to the first tendrils of private hair. He rises to fill my hand. I'm so grateful I'm blinking back tears. This is how it was. The one thing we've salvaged from four years so good we couldn't imagine an end. Little waves lapping. Something blurs. Don't stop. My GOD, Kevin. There's a noise from one of the cribs, adadadadadada daah, loud and steady with a tiny edge of complaint, but we ignore it. I love you. You. Nothing is irrevocable. But it's both of them now, Seth and Simon in unison, loud urgent bleats aaaannh! aaaannh! aaaannh! aaaannnh! "How about this, Kevin? I'll get one and you get one?"

"Jeeezus Christ!"

"I'm sorry, honey."

He flings the covers aside and hurls himself out of bed.

Milk

The crying is frantic now. No time to put clothes on. I grab a boy in each arm and lurch downstairs; manage to take a bottle out of the refrigerator without strangling or dropping anyone. I tip the bottle up for Simon, raising Seth's head to my breast in the crook of my arm. Seth gets the good stuff because he's been whimpery lately. He cries when I leave the room, sometimes when I merely turn my back—his awareness of the awful possibilities seems to have dawned already. He's okay now though, sucking in hard, even tugs while his hand feels its way into my mouth. The refrigerator warms to my bare back. Now it's almost right. It's how I felt in the hospital when they wheeled in the twins for their first feeding. My roommate had her one nice little baby but I was surrounded by babies, filled up with babies—nothing in my mind but the smell of sour milk and the sweet smell that comes from bald baby heads. This house (a hunting cabin built by Kevin's brother) is in the Wisconsin wetlands, full of cranberry bogs and birds and mosquitoes, and right now I could die here, sink right down in the cranberry bog of motherhood. Chrissie Hynde comes on in the living room, a song from her album *Learning to Crawl* that she made the year her kid was born. Kevin comes into the kitchen and hand-grinds our coffee. I feel the muscles in my face relaxing. I want to make Kevin happy. If he's happy, then all of us, Seth, Simon, and me, we can all be happy. "Come here and put your arms around us."

"My arms aren't long enough."

"Please, Kevin, I want you."

"You don't get everything you want in this world."

"Which means what?"

"Which means? You have just what you want! And I don't have what I want! So get off my fucking back!"

"But I *don't* have what I want. I want—" But I can't say "you" because he'd feel even more put-upon. And I can't yell back because then there'd be two angry people. I want to say, "If you'd just take some responsibility," but he'd accuse me of preaching. Or, "Why don't you go out and get a job?," but we moved out here so he could work full-time on his songs. My head is crammed with all the things I'm not allowed to say bumping up against each other, filling all the space so there's no room for thinking. "We've got to stop this."

"We can't stop anything, Debra. We're on the train. The babies are in charge now."

"We can control our manners. How we talk to each other."

"Maybe."

"You know, Kevin, it might help if you got a part-time job, something in a nice environment like that music store you used to work at. Or if you got your band together again. You could write in the morning and we'd have money for child care, maybe get to see a movie or something together."

My words hit some hard thick part of him and bounce back to me. I wish I had my clothes on. I am naked in every way. I'm piti-ful—alone, unloved and helpless with my poor little babies. Then it's gone. I see his back bare, thin and red-blotched where it lay on the wrinkled sheet and *it* looks pitiful. And I don't care. "Have it your way, don't get a job! *I'll* get a job!"

"None of this is my way."

I feel strong in a way that hurts my throat. But strong enough to ignore him.

. . .

Milk

OPEN UP, SETH. Newspaper tastes good, yes? But don't swallow it. Jesus, your face. How many times have I told you, go for the good stuff, nice clean telephone message paper. Behave and I'll give you daddy's music writing paper, yum yum, those skinny little stripes—You think that's funny do you? Now let's get serious. Come sit on momma's lap, help momma find a good job. Find AEROBICS, momma taught aerobics a long time ago before you were born, a nice job so where are the A's? Seth, goddammit! Seth, how could you? You would go after just what momma wants, you asshole baby, how is momma going to put all these pieces together again, you bad bad gorgeous baby you mmmmm you smell good. Mmmm you cutie pie. Come on, don't cry. Shuh, shuh. I don't care about AEROBICS. AEROBICS bore me, point to something on this page. BANK AND FINANCE. Yeah, sure. And it's got to be nights. Daddy writes in the daytime so momma works nights. BEAUTICIAN. Sweetheart, you have to understand momma has no experience in anything. Momma took voice lessons. Piano lessons. Dancing—ballet, tap, toe. A Bachelor's in Dance, Dean's List two semesters. But where's the Dean when I need him? Where's that List, did you eat the list? Now that's supposed to be funny. Learn to laugh at the right time, will you? And look under BALLET. Or DANCER. That's right, drool all over DANCER. Because I need your honest baby-opinion—would you like to see your momma as a go-go dancer? Think about it. How would it feel telling the other babies your momma works at *Bubbles and Broads?* Or *Belles-on-Their-Toes?* Clever, huh? Rings on her fingers and bells on her toes, get it? Get it, you brilliant baby? Now tell me the truth. You won't miss your momma too much? You won't cry when nasty daddy gives you dinner and not your nice momma? You better not cry, or I'll cry. I don't want to leave you a second, you and your gorgeous brother, no no no no no, but some things in life– You'll see. *Les Girls. Norm, 2–4 p.m.* There are a bunch here. Come on, sweet, let go, momma needs the address.

EVERYONE IS BLOND in the Twin Cities. Squint your eyes and that's what you see, yellow-white, skin and hair. Squint in New York and you get mud, a mix. Kevin stood out at NYU with all those dark-haired New Yorkers but here he blends in. Kevin Johnson. There are forty pages of Johnsons in the Twin Cities phone book, like Smith or Jones in Eastern cities.

I do not blend in. I am–I feel it as I walk down these streets– downright swarthy. Is that why the manager of *Bubbles and Broads* does not ask me to take my blouse off?

The sign outside said TOPLESS in orange neon. The manager, Al Peterson, has a little round grape of a nose, and wispy pale hair that shows the pink of his scalp. He looks like my husband grown soft and old. I gave him my maiden name, Debra Lowenthal. He says, "Sorry, Debbie," as if he's doing me a favor by turning me down.

I am from New York, I tell him in my mind–worse things have happened to me than taking my clothes off in front of a stranger. Once, before I was developed enough for a bra, my second cousin rubbed one of my breasts under my T-shirt. It felt too dirty to tell my mother. Once, on the way up from the subway, a man unzipped his pants, pointed inside, and said, "You want?" Are these terrible things? They felt terrible at the time.

Les Girls is down the street from *Bubbles* and a bit flashier. The sign outside is a neon leg cut off at the thigh that jerks up, then kicks, jerks, kicks. On both sides of the door are glassed-in pictures of Lusty Laura and Hot Helen of Joy. Downstairs, though, does not continue the sleaze motif. On every flat surface is a stuffed fish, the largest maybe eight-feet long with a plaque underneath: Oren "Buddy" Anderson caught this prize-winning marlin in 1943. I'm not crazy about taxidermy but it's a homey touch in a burlesque hall. Other reassurances: The carpet looks vacuumed. The stage is raised up above the floor and equipped with real curtain and footlights. The only person in the room, a guy writing at the bar, has a sweet, boy's face—small features, small gestures, something tender in the way he gets off the stool and holds out his hand to me. I say, "My name is Chrissie Anderson." In the light I see that his skin is marked all over with faint crisscrossing lines, his face, his hands. From across the room he'd looked twenty years old. Close up he is forty-five. "I saw your ad."

"Yes indeedy."

"I'm looking for Norm."

"Ah, yes, Norm." He holds my hand for a beat longer than he has to and he doesn't say whether he's Norm or not. But I'm comforted by his voice. It's distinctly not threatening, as if he's gay or English. "You've waited tables before?"

"I was looking, actually, for a dancing job. You advertised dancing."

"It's a special kind of dance we do here, love."

His voice has turned broad. Cockney English, street-class, as if he's trying to scare me. "I've done all kinds of dancing," I say. "I don't have any experience as a waitress."

"Or striptease experience either. But I bet y' know how to take your clothes off. Okay, you talked me into it."

Before I can think yes or no I'm standing on the stage watching him run up a circular iron staircase at the back of the room. Then I can't see anything. The room is gone, chairs, tables. There's a wall of light so bright my eyes water. Music too loud to make out the words. It quiets to the lowest level of painful, becomes a female voice, a song from a musical my mother liked. I'm rummaging for the name when I hear from on high: "All right, Christie!" Okay, I'm Christie now. I'm All Right. I'm a vocalist with a Brooklyn accent and a great range, I can go high and low equally forte: *Take back the mink. Take back the poils. What made you think— That I was one of those goils—?* and then I'm no one I know dancing a dance I've never seen, that I just invented, a little modern, a little jazz, some stuff I used to do at fraternity parties, swimming mixed with bobbing for apples. This isn't bad. The singer is belting it out now, pummeling her lover with her resounding righteous anger, and I feint left, right, left, slowly because my breasts are full. They move slowly, left, right, left, counterweighting my body like the fins of a marlin. I feel limber, strong. The music stops. The voice from on high has a colder edge: "What y' waitin' for, love. Easter?" He says "Easter" like "oyster."

"Sorry," I say. "No previews."

He is downstairs, a shadow behind the footlights but his voice is surprisingly loud. "Come now, love. How do you expect me to hire y' without I know what y' can do?"

"Try me one night."

"This is a joke, right?"

"Norman," I say in my sleaziest voice, "I take my clothes off when I'm paid to take my clothes off."

I'm intrigued with my new persona. His eyes on my chest don't bother me. I stick myself out a little farther. It starts now, the first prickles of letdown. I haven't nursed in going on five hours.

"You look a bit young."

"I've always looked young."

"What I mean is." He looks at my face now, and I stare right back, sucking in my cheeks to make me look older. "We've a clientele here. They are not schoolboys. They have a drink, a good time, they forget their manners."

I stare back without blinking. I can take bad manners.

"My daughter, if I had a daughter, which I don't, would not be working here."

I look bored with Norm's hypothetical daughter.

"You do three sets, the first two with G-string. Then it all comes off."

I smile at him.

"Well," he says, "if everything's here that appears to be here we're in for a bit of a treat."

AT HOME "Learning to Crawl" is on the tape deck. Kevin is on the living room couch watching the "MacNeil-Lehrer News Hour" with the sound off. MacNeil moves his crooked, sensitive mouth while the words warble around the room: *Nobody's perfect, not even a perfect stranger–* I pick Seth up. He has been rubbing what looks like milky spit up into the mirror on his Activity Center. Simon grins at me, rocking back and forth on his hands and knees. Kevin lifts his head as if he can just barely, then sinks back down. My breasts are hard as rocks; they ache as I tell him my story.

"No," he says, "I don't mind it that you got that sort of job. I mean, if that's what you want to do— No, I don't mean that's what you want to do like it's your life goal or something but if that's the job you have for now I don't feel it's my place— Why are you look- ing like that? You make me think I got the wrong answer or some- thing. Okay, to tell you the truth I'm not crazy about my wife strut- ting around naked in front of a roomful of horny creeps, who would, but what can I say, you're of age. Deb, what's the matter? Usually I can't shut you up. Debra, come on."

I'm watching Simon rock back and forth. He's my social baby. He wants to be over here where these voices are but he hasn't figured out how to make his hands work with his feet. He's not upset, though. He rocks faster and faster. His knees leave the ground. "You could try picking up one of your hands," I say to Simon.

"Do you want me to come the first night, Debra? Tell me the truth. Do you want me there for moral support or something?"

I'm thinking about Kevin at NYU. I was crazy about him. I felt weak when I walked into a club where he was playing. His voice was wrong for rock, he said, too sweet. I loved his voice.

"Debra, please. I'm stupid. You have to spell it out for me."

One New Year's while we were making love he dialed my parents' house in Scarsdale and gave me the phone. I could barely say Happy New Year. My father kept saying, Is something wrong, Debbie?

Milk

"Don't make me feel like a jerk. Come on, honey, it's that number again."

He still looks beautiful to me. Eyes. Hands. A nice thickness of forearm though he does not work out, sometimes can barely lift a spoon. "What's there to spell out, Kevin? That you don't know? That you'd change? Instead of the subject?"

"Deb, honey, you don't have to do this job if you don't want to."

I start and abort several statements. There is this tightness in my throat and behind my eyes. "Do you forbid me?" I say.

"How can I forbid you?" he says.

I walk over to Simon who has somehow receded from us. He is wedged under the telephone table on the far side of the room. He looks at me to find out how to react. Scream, Simon. I pick him up but he turns his head away from my chest. I try Seth. He isn't interested either.

"Did you just feed them, Kevin? I hope you didn't feed them."

It wasn't Kevin's fault; they were hungry; they had cried. Almost in tears I sit down at the kitchen table and start hand-expressing my milk into a mixing bowl. *Nobody's perfect, not even a perfect gent. When your property took the A-train, I wonder where your manners went–* The milk comes out in a fine, hard, multidirectional spray that sometimes misses the side of the bowl and hits the refrigerator across the room.

WHEN I GET BACK from my first night it's 3 A.M. but Kevin has waited up. He has done some other nice things, put out a bottle of brandy on the kitchen table with two little snifters we took from a bar near our old apartment.

"You're lusting after me, Kevin."

He laughs. "I've been worried about you." He keeps staring at me; he won't take his eyes off my face, as if I'd gone in for a nose job or something.

"Nothing different," I say. "Same old Debra Lowenthal. They bill me as Krysta Kleen, by the way. I'm going to tell them to call me Krysta K. Kleen. I'll come out in a sheet. With swastika-pasties."

"It went okay?"

"It went."

"And the audience?"

"Your basic horny creeps."

"What about the other acts?"

"Worse than mine."

"How worse?" He's leaning across the table toward me. He wants to devour this stuff.

"Two of them writhe around together like lesbians, pretending to feel each other up. Another one straddles this chair–"

"Like lesbians? Just pretending, though. They're not touching, are they?"

"You're right. You're absolutely right."

He laughs the way I laugh when he makes a joke at my expense. Harder. He's excited, exhilarated. He fills the snifters, drips brandy onto the table. "And how are you?"

"About to drop dead."

"Not yet. Please. What was it like, dancing in front of those brutes?"

Milk

"Do you mean, was it erotic?"

"Is that what I mean?"

"It was the opposite of erotic."

He moves behind me and starts massaging my shoulders. I have been hating him, I feel that now. I feel hate under my skin like hard wax, the hate breaking up a little under his fingers. Yes, I need this. Yes. More. There are tears suddenly, large enough to fall out of my eyes onto the back of my hands. I turn to kiss his arm, feel the wet from my cheek against the little hairs. His hands move down my shoulders across my chest. This is not what I want. No, please. Please, I'm tired. I think this as loud as I can, hoping it'll occur to him. Hoping he'll come upon it as his idea. He has my blouse off, he spreads me out on the living room rug like a sheet cake, nibbling away at the salmon lipstick that heightens the pink of the nipples.

"That's sort of disgusting, Kevin."

"It tastes great."

A small whimper, sharp and clear from upstairs. I feel the milk come. I picture Seth and Simon, the little perfect bows of their mouths. "I should get them."

"Mmmmmmm."

I close my ears to the sound while I chant to myself, Mmmmm, yes, but I'm thinking, I smell, I've got to shower. I'm telling myself, God, that feels good! but I keep hearing a voice from a table up front, Come sit on my face. And it wasn't the words that bothered me, though they aren't words I want to keep thinking about–it was the face I saw later from the wing. The head, almost bald, just a fringe of pale red on a skull round like an egg. Round like the heads of my twin baby boys. And the picture of my babies in their cribs with their large perfect fuzzy round heads destroys my whole small store of sexual momentum.

"I can't now. I'm sorry."

"I'm sorry, too."

He sounds tight-mouthed and young but my heart is beating so fast it's hard to breathe.

Upstairs it's a little better. The boys are asleep now, Simon curled around his set of plastic keys, Seth on his back with one arm flung over his head. I pick Seth up. His eyes are closed, but he comes at the breast with his mouth open wide, smiling. "Seth, you darling. You crazy boy." I let him nurse and nurse till he's asleep again, his little mouth quiet and hidden under the curve of breast.

WHEN WE FIRST MOVED up here I was in my second trimester, the best part of pregnancy—I wasn't sick anymore and I could turn over in bed. Kevin wrote in the morning while I taught low-impact to senior citizens at the Grantsburg Fitness Center. Then all afternoon and into the evening we'd play uncomplicated games together, Scrabble, gin rummy, cribbage, things that tickled your mind but you didn't care if you won or lost. Days passed like clothes on the line rippling in a steady wind.

Now I don't notice how the days pass. Is Kevin happy? Are the boys happy? They laugh sometimes. They weigh what they're supposed to weigh. And Kevin complains less. At least he complains to me less. At least I don't remember Kevin complaining.

What I mostly remember in the two-day spans between my

shows is my backyard in a suburb of New York City, where in the warm late spring I would lie on a chaise longue under our crab apple tree and watch the bits of sky through the leaves and branches. I also remember the wall of light between myself and the *Les Girls* audience, a dizzying, rainbow-colored blur like the halo around lights after you've been swimming in chlorine. And the round-head, the Humpty Dumpty, who came again and sat where he had sat before, at the table to the far right. "He's a fan," Norm said. "Y' c'd take it as a compliment." But in my dream that night he was trying to force me onto a bus with CHARTER above the windshield, a red bus with black seats, red and black, the colors that if you wore them in high school on Friday, meant you were a whore. Of course no big deal. But I keep thinking, what if he asks me out and I say no and he's enraged. So now I park against the back wall with Norm waiting at the door till I'm in the car and away, though he's getting tired of it, I can tell. Last night he told me I was overdoing the fear thing, and I couldn't explain it right, which is fine. Norm is Norm. Norm is the norm, he's not my friend or my father. Still, I wanted him to know I wasn't afraid the guy would rape me. I'd already imagined that—it wouldn't kill me. But it's the sight and sound of him. I want him gone from my world, that thick white Humpty Dumpty whispering loud so people will think we have a thing going, whispering to me like some telephone pervert when I go to his side of the stage, "Those bazooms. I love those bazooms." Saying, "Lean down here, Krysta honey. I got my mouth open. I'm ready to suck that pretty pink bazoomba all the way down my throat."

There's a limit, isn't there? Even I have a limit. I told Norm I couldn't dance stage right with him sitting there but Norm said I was supposed to entertain both sides of the room equally. "They paid their money, y' know, love. Y'll have to shut your sweet ears."

YOU BOUGHT ME the fur coat five winters ago
  And the gown the following fall.
  The jacket, the gloves, the shoes, and the hat
  Were your generous gifts, I recall.
  But last night in your apartment
  You tried to remove them all
  And I screamed as I ran down the hall—

I have danced to this song so many nights it runs through my head on the drive home, in the bathroom when I brush my teeth. It's louder than the crickets in the woods around our house, louder than the two crickets that have made their home in the loose pine paneling behind my dresser. It's waiting for me when I wake up in the morning, echoing along highway seventy, route thirty-five back to the Cities, *Take back the mink. Take back the pearls. What made you think—that I was one of those girls? I'm dreamin'!* so that when I prance out onto the stage in my heels, cloak, and filmy skirt it's as if I've been dancing all day, as if I'm one of the twelve princesses who sneaked out from the palace every night and danced their dainty shoes to ribbons. I'm tired the way I was tired the first month after the babies were born, so tired I don't even feel bad—I'm floating in a thin soup, seeing the world through a veil over my face—and it's true, I have a veil over my face, a white bridal veil with sequins that glitter in the colored light. A veil that hides me, closes out the eyes of the audience so that intentionally, as an act of pure free will I tear it off, clap it once to my chest, then fling it out over the footlights without feeling anything at all. *Take back the gown, the shoes, and the hat. I may be down... But I'm not flat as all that!*

But when the veil is gone I feel its absence. I move faster, more wildly, as if speed, as if the sweat on my body will stand in for the clothes I'm removing. Satin cloak. I waltz it round and round and round the stage, then ball it up and kick it into the wings with the pointy toe of my high heel shoe. I still have my skirt on. I love my skirt, how it clings to my legs, flares out as I twirl. But it too will go. I kick once front, once back, I unhook.

Now all I have on is a string with a hankie between and my gold halter. I need an upper for this, and Norm has thoughtfully provided it, a 25-mg biphetamine called Black Beauty, that turns me for twenty minutes into Cleopatra, Godiva, a magnificent woman who makes her own rules. I unhook in front, then turning my back to the audience I take off the bra and shake it—there's an actual gasp. They're mine now. I flaunt my bare back, twirl my bit of sparkly gold; I do what I want. I cajole them, torture them, turning front, back, front, back, and in back the top is off, dangling, but every time I turn front it miraculously covers me, and then at last when I'm sure the orthodontist from Duluth will fall over dead on his little round table, I turn front, kiss each half of the gold brassiere and hold it up over my head. I look like a politician. I look like a victim in a holdup. I am uncertain as to how I look. The pill is wearing off.

It's hot here on stage. Oven hot, sun-on-cement hot. The lights hurt my eyes, the big spot from the booth on the far wall turning me red blue yellow green, red blue yellow green. The red burns at me, melting the makeup off my face, my skin, melting my skin. I feel my skin melting, running down my face till I have less on than a stripper is allowed to have on. I have my little flesh-colored string with the hankie between, I have my gold nipple-stars with the tassles I have learned to twirl clockwise, then reverse, then toward each other like gears, though I'm so large and heavy with milk I hurt climbing the stairs not to mention twirling my pasties, but it's okay, it's still okay—till I hear my Humpty Dumpty, my bargain basement demon rapist lover: "Let me rub those bazooms, Krysta baby. Let me rub my cock between those bazooms." I walk over to where the sound is coming from, singing along with the record, *So take back the mink...From whence it came. And tell 'em to shorten the slee-eeves*— I peel off my shiny stars, take my breasts in both hands like a pair of sixguns and squirt down in the direction of the voice.

As the foots die and the house lights come on I see Norm walking up the aisle toward me. But I'm fixed on Humpty, his eyes disturbingly wide apart, his wide, flabby mouth, which has compressed and frozen into a little O. Norm is standing next to me. He wants me off the stage, out of his place, his life, now! I want that too, God, yes! I want to drive home, feed the babies. But the silence has caught me, the sounds you hear in silence—the light static of speakers with the music off, the rough breathing of men who snore, and behind all this, far away and barely audible, the thin wail of a newborn baby. Is there a baby in the house? I scan the audience, men of many ages and sizes, heavy-shouldered and scrawny-necked, slack-jowled and lean-jawed, in suits, jean jackets and message T-shirts, but with the same blond face, and I think I see in the sea of faces one that looks like Kevin's.

Or maybe not. They all look like Kevin, looking up at me with their mouths in that same little O—like fish that have swallowed a hook, like frantic babies hunkering for their milk.

❧ Polio ❧

The whole trip, Noah's been playing with the quarters I gave him for cleaning his room. Aaron thinks it's cute. Our son loves money the way kids his age love dogs. There's a tenderness. Aaron and I joke about this yuppie kindergartner supporting us in our old age, his identity crisis sending him not to Baba Ram Dass, with whom Aaron spent a post-college year, but to Harvard Business School. Speech, which came slow to Noah, decidedly later than to all my girlfriends' children, still squeezes out like old glue, but he knows if ten Nintendos cost a thousand dollars, two thousand will buy twenty. This is what I remind myself as I think of Laura's son calling her Laura at fifteen months (he still does, though she admits to preferring Mom), as my son loses one of his coins into the mysterious inner reaches of the seat and starts sobbing as though his feelings are hurt. "What do you want, Noah?" I say, although of course I know what he wants. "If you want me to help you with something, you could ask me."

His grief goes on as if I hadn't said anything. I wonder for the thousandth time if he's hard of hearing, though he's been tested. If

I've gone crazy. Air blows through the car damp and hot enough to make you crazy, from Noah working the power windows. "Do you want me to look for your quarter, Noah? Try this: 'Mom, could you help me find that quarter?' Hey, and roll that up, will you?"

He looks at me with eyes wide open, wounded and hopeless like a refugee child. Hot wind whips his hair. When I was Noah's age we called it polio wind, throbbing with germs—we had to go inside and lie down—but I unbuckle, turn. My jacket constricts me, and I take it off, still smoky, I notice, from Phyllis, our paralegal, who can't think without a cigarette in her hand. I pull my blouse out of my skirt, stretch between the front bucket seats toward the crumb-dusty crotch of backseat and seatback. There's a Lego block, chewed unusable. The plastic arm of a Ninja Turtle. I pull my skirt to my hips, kick off my shoes, hoist myself onto the floor in back, reach under both front seats and the mats. Noah's breathing is calmer, an occasional flutter, soothed by my work on his behalf. "Aaron, could you pull over a minute? I think it fell between the seat and the door."

"You're nuts, Joanie."

"I know that. Could you stop anyway?"

"It's late," he says. "I don't want to start setting up in the dark."

"Please, Aaron. We have flashlights. And Laura's bringing the Coleman."

"And if *they're* late?"

"They left this *morn*ing! Come on, how long could it take?"

He doesn't argue, but doesn't stop either. Noah's breath flutters with the push-pull of our argument. I'm not a winner of verbal arguments. In my firm I'm the least senior attorney, least able, I think sometimes, though on other days I assess more reasonably: My briefs are cogent, persuasive, for the most part. I do not go to trial.

Under pressure I lose every vestige of grace. Six years ago, in heavy labor with Noah not coming and not coming, I'm asking, please, for a C-section, and my ob-gyn, her strong hands on my arms, is going, "Push! Push!" and Aaron, who happens to be a pediatrician: "You can do it, honey!" And I don't want to but I push; for Dr. Salzman and natural childbirth, for Aaron, weeping, I push. Then, in the course of the surgery, which I had anyway hours later because of Noah's "brow presentation," a position that, were I more spiritually inclined, I'd see as his grail or his karma—he must somehow learn to tuck his chin—Noah emerges with one side of his forehead bloody-swollen. Salzman looks neutral, as if this is one of a delivery's many normal variants. But when Noah falls sweetly asleep on my shoulder, my first, last, and only baby, I think of his soft infant skull under its fuzz of skin knocking and knocking against the closed doors of my pelvis, and my legs shake with the thought, although it might be the anesthetic, and I tell Salzman under my breath, If you hurt *one* of his perfect brain cells I'll sue the living shit out of you, so help me God! But of course I haven't. After all, I'd listened to her.

Now I open my purse, hand Noah a new quarter. He takes a breath, assessing the plea-bargain. "'Thanks, Mom,'" I say.

"Thanks, Mom."

Aaron rolls his eyes. Hot wind blows the sweat off my face and makes more sweat, at the same time. But Noah's face is so radiant I'm not sorry I gave in to him.

. . .

WE ARRIVE in the luminous purple of just after sunset. They've chosen well, a site more tree-lined than the others in this section, with a two-man tent to our right and no one to our left, minimal hindrance to our enjoyment of the Wisconsin Park Bureau version of nature.

In the shadow of the raised trunk, amid the whine of mosquitoes, I put on jeans and a T-shirt. I fold my office clothes, their odors of smoke and deodorant, into a Jewel bag. Stretch my arms, take a breath of darkening air. It smells like grass, dirt, trees. Underlay of manure. I like the smell of manure. There's a flash of the time before husband, child. Before puberty, maybe. The crack-open of possibility.

Over the picnic table hangs our friends' Coleman, too bright for the twilight woods, bright as the light in a diner. You can see the seams of bathing suits as they dry down the sides of the tent, you see the terry burr of towels, their stripes in the gaslight supernaturally distinct, Martian-colored. At one end of the table a bottle of wine and a bottle of ketchup gleam coldly. I watch from the dark beyond, Jake seated under the lantern, pretending to read the newspaper. Or maybe he's really reading it, precocious six-year-old. His father Dan is building a fire inside the site's metal ring. Maya, three, hobbles toward him with a branch too big for her. Dan takes the branch, praises it elaborately. Good dad, good guy, running to help Aaron with the gear, placing on his cheeks a pair of formal kisses from a system of manners that has always charmed me. Laura sets down a bucket to give Aaron a thin-armed hard hug. We've known Laura as long as anyone in Chicago that we're still friends with, having met ten years ago in a Zen meditation group we've all discontinued. At times I think I admire her more than I like her, but I do like her. She's smart, funny, and frank. And beautiful in a New York way, noisy earrings and slim pants on long, long legs, wispy curls framing high cheekbones. She can be brusque; there's an edge sometimes, especially with Dan. Her practice is shallow, Aaron said once, in the language of the time. Still she does *zazen* every morning, thirty minutes facing the wall before leaving for her and Dan's café, which offers occult books along with natural foods. Right now she pulls from the bucket ears of what must be organically grown corn, arranging them on the grill with mindless grace, no disjunction between what she thinks and what she does.

Dan and Aaron begin to set up our tent. Laura looks around for something; me, of course. I should join them, I think. What is this hanging back? But I'm watching as through a window, Noah dancing around Jake at the picnic table. Noah peers at what Jake's reading, jumps back, seemingly electrified by the close presence of this child who in the past has been disdainful and at times downright rude to him. Noah isn't thinking of this as he plants himself behind the older boy, puts his hands over Jake's eyes. Guess who? I look up at the sky turning black, not wanting to see Jake pulling away with an annoyed flick of the head. Jake finds a seat at the other end of the site from this strange boy, this little jerk (Jake's term) who doesn't seem to know what a six-year-old—first grader come fall—is supposed to know. Jake is only six months older but has a strong clear will, his declarations as assured as a preteen's. Sometimes he makes fun of Noah's slow speech, repeating some phrase of Noah's in the same cadence and inflection with no rebuke from Laura who believes in noninterference. I say to myself, if the asshole's rude to Noah once more, I'm packing us in the wagon back to Chicago, I don't care what time it is.

Jake sits still with Noah's hands over his eyes. His mouth moves as if he's asking a question. Guessing who? Playing Noah's game?

It isn't a baby game, it's a fine game, worthy of first grade. When Noah releases him, Jake looks at him straight on, as at a respected contemporary. Nods are exchanged. Noah grins. The boys start walking together toward the road. "Hey!" I cry. "Where do you think you're all going?"

Noah looks at me as if he hasn't the faintest idea who I am. Jake says, "We're going to the camp store. It's just past the turn."

I wish it was Noah who spoke so politely and fluently, but I'm warmed by their comaraderie. "Have a good one," I say, stepping into the circle of light to greet my friends.

FOR A WHILE it's simple pleasure, woods, crickets, the sticky heat of the day rising up and away. Marinated tuna steaks hiss on the cooler sides of the grill. If smoke hits your eyes you turn till you hit downwind. Sometimes the smoke dances you round and round the cook, as if it's got your number, but the paranoia feels benign, like teasing. "This is so Zen!" I cry. Everyone laughs.

Turning a slab of tuna Laura says, "Governing a state is like grilling a small fish, Lao Tzu said that."

"*Boil*ing a fish," Aaron says.

"Wasn't that Machiavelli?" I ask giddily.

"Lao Tzu was a fine cook," Dan says. People laugh.

Aaron recites a Zen poem: "Sitting quietly, doing nothing/ Spring comes and the grass grows by itself."

There are long comfortable pauses between comments.

When the boys return from the store Jake's walking fast with Noah scurrying behind like a page. Noah's face is glowing, though, as his trot ends by the camp. He has bought a Blow Pop, his favorite this season, a sucker with a core of bubble gum. He unwraps it, plants it in his mouth, kneels by the fire. I can't see his face but his bent head and hunched shoulders radiate intensity, baby Moses crawling over Pharaoh's straw mat toward the choice that means life or early death. I approach slowly, so as not to startle him. Then I see: His hand is burning. There's a flame. He gazes unblinking, his face the color of fire. "*Noah!*"

My voice is so thin I'm not sure I actually spoke. I rush to my son. It's not his hand on fire but the Blow Pop wrapper he's holding, burning in a supernaturally even line of flame. "Noah, drop that!"

The paper, burning, floats to the ground. Noah's face registers simple amazement. Then his chin crumples. His sucker fell too. Before I can stop him he's reaching into the fire. His wail careens up, bone shocking in the flickering wind. I try to hold him but I'm caught between that and the impulse to run for ice, and I can't move at all. I'm seized up. It's like a dream in which the killer or avalanche is coming, getting larger out of the corner of your eye, and your legs freeze. As if from the top of a hill I stare down at my son with his hand in his mouth. He screams at the fire.

Laura hurries over with a wet rag. Aaron brings the flashlight. The pads of two of Noah's fingers have begun to turn white, but his tears are for the ashy Blow Pop. Shaking with relief, I run for the First Aid, uncap the ointment. Apply nervously more than is needed. Aaron cuts the gauze with the little scissors from his Swiss Army knife, binds Noah's fingers. He tosses Noah into the air, sets him down. Noah wants a new Blow Pop but the store has closed now. With Aaron's knife and a spatula I retrieve what's left of the sucker. "I'll rinse it off for you."

"New chapter," Aaron says. "Time to move on."

Noah looks from me to Aaron and back again, shifting between the muck of my overanxiousness and the falseness of Aaron's cheer. Seated on the cooler, Jake rips open a corner of his own snack, a packet of something that comes with a tiny spoon. Noah chooses Jake—not walking but gliding, eliding, as if drawn by a power beyond will. He gravitates. "Could I have some?" he asks in the polite, well-modulated voice of a child you don't have to worry about.

"Say *please,* Noah," I say.

"Please," he says automatically. Then, smiling at me: "It's a Fun-Dip. I bought him it with my own money! Twenty-five cents plus tax!" He concludes with an excited little bounce. Jake, though, seems unaware of him. Jake's spoon moves from packet to mouth. Jake licks his lips.

"Jake," Noah says, "could I have a taste of your Fun-Dip, please Jake?"

Maya walks over to Jake with her mouth open like a baby bird. He doles her some of the sweet powder. "Me too!" Noah says with some urgency. Jake sinks lower into his packet. I look around for help but Aaron and Dan are staking the tent. Laura is close enough to have heard but she remains oblivious. It's what her Zen has turned into, noninterference in the social behavior of her children. "Ja-ake?" Noah says, tugging at his sleeve.

"You have germs." Jake raises the packet to his lips for a long proprietary swallow, then walks over to his mother, folding down the open corner. "Laura," he says, "save this for me." Laura takes the packet. Noah looks confused. You little shit, I say to Jake under my breath. You six-year-old slimeball. But Noah has already backed away, dazed by the rebuff he has no words to challenge.

My arms and legs feel stiff, my brain gray fuzz. Ladies and gentlemen of the jury, is this supposed to be good for him? An experience from which adult self-assurance derives? I imagine Laura: *feeling these small pains now will help him handle them later on,* and Aaron's misapplied Zen boiling down to *everything we do will only make it worse,* not Zen but laissez-faire parenting, survival of the fittest, which means of the nastiest, least sensitive, psychologically least vulnerable—regard *Lord of the Flies,* oh wise, discerning jurypeople—but Aaron's voice in my head drowns out the voice that says *give Jake a kick in the teeth,* and I remember the girl who moved into the house across the street when I was five, who'd had what was called infantile paralysis. She'd spent a month in an iron lung, my mother said, and I felt sick to my stomach, having seen magazine pictures of a vault on little crib wheels, a custom-made prison cell certain children were consigned to for not taking a nap in the hot afternoon or going swimming too soon after lunch, inscrutable justice of the universe. This girl, whose name was Darlene, I remember, had emerged from her cell. But she wore metal splints to hold her legs straight and she lurched along the sidewalk, her head turned hard to one side, as if listening for a near-inaudible instruction—it made me gag in the back of my throat. Her arms didn't swing back and forth like other people's but rather shot out suddenly, randomly. The thumb and forefinger of both her hands were pinched together as if she were holding teacups. Once she fell down in the middle of her driveway, a heap of limbs and metal sticks, and I stood on my side of the street with my hands over my eyes not just because I wasn't allowed to cross but because, if I touched her, I thought, I'd end up in an iron lung. I stood there crying till her mother walked out the door. Later in my backyard I tried to see how fast I could move walking like her, leading with my side, circling my stiff wobbly legs.

Now, though, I regather enough of myself to track Noah down. "Jake's a turd," I say conspiratorially, putting my arm around him. He bears my embrace more from compassion for me, it seems, than from any comfort he derives. With Aaron's pocketknife I butter him an ear of corn. He eats it.

AFTER DINNER we settle all three children into Laura and Dan's tent. Jake makes no objection. Noah is calm, a little remote, a cross between a zombie and a yogi. As they nestle in sleeping bags Dan tells them a ghost story he made up that's scary enough to satisfy without inducing nightmares. We've given them two small flashlights, and as the tale proceeds they run the lights over the ceiling of the tent, taking turns like angel children. Giggles and murmurs flow from the tent even after we've zipped them in. From time to time one of us strides over from the camp and tries ineffectually, congenially, to quiet them down. Aaron and Laura are right, I tell myself. I must learn to trust the spirit of growth in Noah. All will be well if I can keep from interfering. Raising a child is like boiling a small fish.

We're all easier now. On the verge of buoyant. Laura can't find her matches so we sojourn to the station wagon to light our joint. It moves from hand to hand, a faint red eye glowing in blackness. My wheel of thoughts slows down, thins out. Laura does not tell us how quickly Jake's learning the piano or how many friends have asked him to sleep over. She describes the ethics lesson Jake gave Maya the other day on what behavior would send her to hell. It included lying to parents and spitting dinner food out into the toilet. "Where did he learn about hell?" Laura asks but not as if she cares. Our voices float in the dark, removed from our selves. "Dan told him he'd go to hell if he didn't practice the piano."

In her tone is something metallic. Dan doesn't respond though. Aaron says, for Dan, "Why do you think he practices the piano?"

I nod at Aaron through the dark. "Everyone knows about hell," I say. "It's genetically transmitted. Like the poop jokes kids bring home from preschool!"

We laugh.

We leave the car for the cool, starry night, talking about the nature of hell outside Catholicism. In Judaism it's Sheol, but no one in my family seemed to worry about it. Hell was bad luck on earth—boils, business losses, and early death. It's fun to talk about hell with the air so damp, balmy. I lie back on Aaron's lap and look for shooting stars in the arena of sky inside the ring of trees.

For the Hindus hell was just another stage in life's slow journey

toward understanding, more painful than earth but just as tempo-
rary, from which you emerge when your evil deeds are burned
away. The ancient Greeks had their Tartarus with poor Tantalus
and Sisyphus, but for the most part their underworld was like a
rainy Sunday with nothing to do. Persephone visits for six months.
There are pomegranate trees. In rare instances, if you plead well
like Orpheus, you are permitted to retrieve a loved one.

A second joint is lit, this time in the embers of the camp.
Sometimes grass deadens me, pushes me deep into a vault of shyness and mental fatigue, but this stuff feels light and airy. The talk
becomes urgent in a pleasant way—our own descents into Hades,
acts of personal heroism or craziness.

Laura describes how once she jumped on the back of a guy, a
stranger, who was beating up his girlfriend. It was night on sleazy
Wells Street. She'd pulled the guy's hair, poked him in the eye; she'd
never dream of doing it now. The woman she rescued was more
surly than grateful, as if Laura had been messing with her man.

"Nutsoid," Aaron says. But I can tell he's impressed.

Dan starts his own hero story. I think of car trips with my family, me practicing in my mind how, if we had an accident—these
were preseatbelt days—I'd put my arms around my younger sister,
of whom I was intensely jealous, and save her from crashing
through the windshield. Later in therapy I dreamed I carried my
hefty shrink down fourteen flights of the building in which he practiced, damp towels over our heads.

When it's my turn I tell about a night in Florida in a furnished
kitchenette my family rented (I was eight or ten) when I walked
into the small living room just as a floor lamp began to topple. I

wanted to run out before the terrible sound of the crash and I wanted to step forward to save the lamp and there seemed to be time to make a reasoned choice because it was all happening so slowly. I watched the lamp fall, graceful as a cut flower, till the white glass bowl and the three peripheral and one center bulb exploded on the thin rented rug.

Everybody laughs. But it's a little hard to breathe. I move deeper into the vault of myself, slowing down and down, till I can't raise my arms and legs. I want the sweater Laura has draped over her shoulders. It's thick Mexican wool. I'd burrow into it. I move closer to the fire but it only warms my hands, my knees. I'm cold, shivering, no strength to keep myself warm.

They rise. Aaron says, "Come to bed, Joanie."

I think of the tent, my down-filled sleeping bag, ready to collect what heat I have and wrap it around me. I want to be there. I imagine myself there. "She's in a trance," Laura says.

"She never gets this high," Aaron says.

"Are you okay, Sweetie?" Laura whispers in my ear.

"I'd like to know what's going on in her mind," Dan says. "She looks blissed out."

"No one says blissed out," Laura says.

"I know that," Dan says. "Do you think I don't know that?"

They smile empathetically at the depth of my bliss. They perhaps envy me. Aaron kisses the top of my head. I sit like a rock, a shoe, as the three tread off to Aaron and my tent. In the darkness an occasional faint giggle flares and winks out. I'm exhausted and know I'll be worse in the morning. I want to lie down with them, leg number four of a table sumptuously spread, but I'm fixed on the fire. Transfixed. If I move, the dry ice of my bones will vaporize leaving me sprawled like a slipcover. In the fire, if I look long enough, is something I need to see.

I'm almost asleep cross-legged on the ground like the Buddha when I become aware of what feels like pressure over my head. It's a presence, a phantom, the ghost that haunts campers. I hold utterly still, focusing on the smoke from the fire as it swirls up to the pool of sky inside our ring of trees. The sky isn't all black, I see. Running across is a smoke-colored streak, that I track down through the trees to the mesh window of the children's tent. How odd. That we are arced by a bridge of smoke. Bridged by an arc of smoke? I'm pleased by my powers of observation, which detect in the arc individual particles of grit. I feel the grit in my eyes and mouth, take a cleansing breath, repress a faint desire to cough. Then it comes clear: The children's tent is on fire. "Aaron!" I scream. "Laura! Dan!!"

Running toward the children's tent I hear coughing, rising wails. "Unzip!" I scream, feeling for the seam in the smoky dark. "Open the zipper! Pull the zipper down!" as if one arrangement of words is better than another.

Commotion mixes with more sustained coughing. I'm fumbling for the zipper tab. Find it under the nylon lip. Blind in the dark, choking, I pull as hard as I can, one hand over the other. The tab comes off in my fingers. The tab is warm. "Mama!" someone cries, I can't tell who. I claw at the tent with my fingernails. "Pull the goddamn zipper! No, stay down! Noah honey, are you in there?!"

. . .

LATER I'LL SIT with Noah on my lap kissing the side of his head as his coughing subsides. Dan and Laura will smile guilty gratitude and I'll smile back as they brush smoke and terror from their children's hair. Aaron will apologize, resolve to smoke no more dope, not that he does much anymore. A teenage girl will appear, stare at us, vanish sometime after I've stopped watching her. On the asphalt parking lot the tent will smolder with a smell of sweet, noxious plastic.

The fire was small, it turns out, the tent fire-resistant. In fact the only thing flammable, we find, is the cotton flannel lining of Jake's and Maya's sleeping bags (Noah's was fire-retardant synthetic), giving off more smoke than flame. We hug and kiss our children till our hearts slow down enough to lay blame. Jake and Noah, it turns out, started it with a box of matches from the family grocery bag. Noah took them. At Jake's bidding. "Stick matches!" Noah says with an utter absence of guilt, in awe of the power unleashed.

"They caught first try," Jake says.

Laura slaps Jake's hand. "I should spank you. Don't you know better than that?!"

"Better than what, Laura?" Jake says.

She slaps him again. Maya starts crying. Jake too. She hugs both of them, laughing crazily. I feel duty bound to punish my son as well but all I can do is kiss his head, his hand, trying to figure out what was different this time, what happened that let me move.

After the zipper broke I started clawing at the tent, the window mesh, but it was like climbing a mountain of glass. I fell to my knees, patting the ground for the lost zipper tab. It was stupid, I knew, another kind of paralysis, but there was no stopping. I was lost with the zipper tab in the stones and sand.

Then, was there a scream? Jake's cry for Mama? There was a steady light wind, as numbing as in the kingdom of dying embers. I did not find the tab. Something bit my hand. It hurt-itched, a wee break in the scheme of things. I floated toward the picnic table, on which I recalled, lucid writer of briefs that I am, the exact placement of Aaron's pocketknife. I remember how it opened to my nimble fingers and sliced through the tent like a scalpel. And how I groped through smoke for the hands of children, anyone's children, since in the hot crackling dark there was no way to tell the difference.

The Author

Sharon Solwitz's literary prizes include a Pushcart Prize, the Dan Curley Award, the Tara Fellowship in Short Fiction (from the Heekin Foundation), the Katherine Anne Porter Fiction Prize, the Nelson Algren Prize (three times), the Hemingway Days Festival Prize, as well as awards and fellowships from the Kansas and Illinois Arts Councils. Her fiction has appeared in such magazines as *Mademoiselle, Ploughshares, American Short Fiction,* and *TriQuarterly.* One of her stories was dramatized in the Stories-on-Stage series at the Organic Theatre in Chicago. Another was selected for radio broadcast in the "Sound of Writing" series. She currently teaches creative writing at Loyola University in Chicago and to public school students as an Artist-in-Education. She edits *Another Chicago Magazine* with her husband, poet Barry Silesky, and takes care of their ten-year-old twin boys.